Number Two

THE RUGBY ZOMBIES

Number Two

DAN ANTHONY

Pont

For

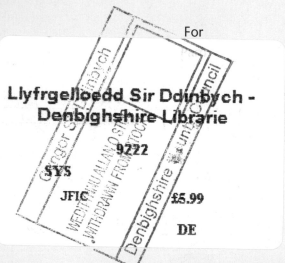

Published in 2011 by Pont Books, an imprint of
Gomer Press, Llandysul, Ceredigion, SA44 4JL

ISBN 978 1 84851 397 6

A CIP record for this title is available from the British Library.

This book is published with the financial support of the
Welsh Books Council.

Printed and bound in Wales at
Gomer Press, Llandysul, Ceredigion

Prologue

Martin pushed a lock of dark hair out of his eyes and watched Arwel plodding down the road. 'Better not bother him for a while,' he said.

'Why?' asked Glen, pulling himself up onto the wall next to Martin. 'I'd say that boy needs intensive therapy, full-on training. His mind's gone. I'd better hit him with sticks.'

'I don't think it's going to help,' said Martin. 'He needs time to get over it.'

'How come?' asked Glen.

'All good players have to deal with losing: you have to know how to lose to work out how to win,' said Martin.

Glen nodded his head: 'That's deep...I don't understand.'

'It's psychology,' said Martin with a patient sigh. 'It's about what's going on in your subconscious mind, and you haven't got one of those.'

Glen thought for a moment. 'If you're saying I'm stupid I'll smash your face in,' he said, still watching Arwel as he reached the end of the road, turned the corner and disappeared from view.

'It means you're less likely to fear the unknown,' said Martin.

Glen nodded. Martin was right about that: he never saw the point of worrying.

Behind them, in the forest, a cold breeze flicked the dark, brittle branches.

Chapter 1

Arwel turned the corner into Constellation Street. He wanted to give it a new name: Disaster Street. As his trainers scuffed the pavement he thought about how things had turned out so terribly wrong.

*

After they'd won the match against Aberscary everybody had believed in him. He and his team of zombies had beaten Aberscary firsts. Not just beaten them, walloped them, smashed them off the field of play.

So with the outside half, Jack Wilson, away from school, Mr Edwards, head of games at Aberscary Comp, had made a bold decision. He had taken Arwel aside after a coaching session to give him the good news. 'Arwel, you're playing at number ten.'

Even at the time, Arwel remembered warning Mr Edwards that he wasn't feeling so good any more.

The coach's brown eyes had jumped about like nervous little beetles. 'You were fantastic when you played against Aberscary,' he said. 'Now I want to see if you can do it for us too – this school needs a winner like you.'

At that moment the flanker, Gilligan, barged past on his way out of the changing room. 'You'd better be good,' he said with a menacing smile, 'and I know you're not.'

'I saw Arwel play,' said Mr Edwards. 'He's brilliant.'

Arwel shifted nervously. When he was playing with the Zombies he had felt lucky, confident, charmed. But now, without them, he felt unlucky, perhaps even cursed.

'Be here tomorrow at half past one ready for the minibus,' said Mr Edwards before disappearing into his office next to the changing rooms.

*

Arwel slowed down. He was walking too fast down Disaster Street. He didn't want to arrive home too soon. He was remembering what had happened next.

*

The ride to Aberlairy had taken about half an hour. There was a strange atmosphere in the school minibus. Mr Edwards drove, sucking nervously on his Tic Tacs. Usually on the way to a game he talked all the time, urging the team to play well, cracking jokes, cheering everybody on with his energy: 'It's a win-win scenario,' he'd say. 'We win or we win – that's what's going to happen.'

But this time his brow was furrowed and he kept his eyes on the road. The drive took longer than usual: there were lots of road works and temporary traffic lights. They had to navigate their way around deep potholes, broken telegraph poles and even an upturned car.

'Must have been a freak storm,' said Glen, who was sitting next to Arwel, 'a twister or something like that.'

'We don't get tornadoes in Aberscary,' said Arwel.

By the time they reached Aberlairy School, Mr Edwards had sucked his way through a whole box of mints. As the boys hopped off the bus he grabbed Arwel's arm. 'Listen, Arwel,' he said. 'I saw you play the other day. You were great.'

Arwel nodded.

'That's why I've put you in at number ten. But now I'm wondering.'

Arwel nodded again; he didn't want to let Mr Edwards down.

'Can I ask you a question?' said the coach.

'No problem,' said Arwel.

'You did play in that game, didn't you? That was you – not some guy who looked like you, or maybe a secret brother, or some relation that looks exactly the same as you . . . but isn't you?'

'It was me,' nodded Arwel.

'You did all that kicking and catching, that passing and tackling and all that point-scoring yourself?'

'Yeah,' said Arwel, nervously.

Mr Edwards straightened his neck. 'Well it's simple then,' he said as he strode towards the rugby pitch.

Arwel followed. 'OK?' he muttered under his breath. 'Do it again!'

The afternoon smelt of winter, the ground was soggy and heavy and the air was filled with fine droplets of water.

It was Arwel's kick-off. He held the ball. He tried to wipe it on his jersey but it slipped and dropped to the floor. He could hear Gilligan sniggering behind him. He could feel the eyes of his team on his back. They wanted him to do well, he knew, but they all thought it was going to go badly.

He drew a deep breath, took the ball in his hands and held it up for the team to see.

'Go on, Arwel!' shouted Glen. 'Welly it!'

Arwel kicked off. Or he tried to. He sliced the ball and it rolled pathetically away to one side.

That was it. Aberlairy had the ball. And they used it well. When they realised Arwel was playing badly they picked him out. They kicked the ball at him and it slipped through his hands. Their pack ran at him . . . and flattened him. And when his scrum half did spin the ball out in his direction, it was so wet and slippery Arwel found he could only just catch it before being tackled by most of the Aberlairy team. He missed all of his touch kicks, all of his penalties and Aberscary Comp lost by 47 points to nil.

Every boy in the team played badly. Glen got sent off for fighting with the Aberlairy forwards. Gilligan got sent off for punching Arwel.

After the game, as they drove home in the minibus, Mr Edwards spoke to the wet, mud-covered boys. 'I've been thinking,' he said slowly, deliberately.

The boys waited.

'Good try, Arwel. You gave it your best shot, one-hundred-and-ten per cent. I thought you tackled like a demon, but that was the only good thing you did . . . In fact, if I'm honest, you were terrible, close to one-hundred-and-eighty per cent in the wrong direction. It was a mistake putting you in at number ten.'

Arwel sat next to Glen with his head in his hands. He nodded slowly. The whole thing had been a nightmare.

'Good riddance to bad rubbish,' hissed Gilligan.

'And you should concentrate on beating up the opposition, not your own team, Gilligan,' said Mr Edwards. 'That's a basic point of principle. Arwel may have played like a zombie but at least he knew who the enemy was.'

Glen patted Arwel on the back: 'Don't worry,' he said. 'Next time we'll really get them.'

*

At home-time Arwel had rushed out of school as fast as he could. He didn't even wait for Glen. He'd gone straight to the only place he knew he'd be safe.

The ground was almost dry in the forest. Arwel's feet bounced slightly on the bed of pine needles. He walked deep into the woods. But there was no cold wind, no icy heart-stopping chill, just this bouncy carpet keeping the pinewood warm and smelling more 'pine fresh' than the stuff his mum squirted around the toilet.

'Delme,' hissed Arwel.

There was no reply.

'Delme!' he shouted.

Arwel heard nothing. He couldn't even smell that weird mushroomy zombie smell. He wandered amongst the trees for a while. But nothing came out to meet him.

When he stepped out of the forest he found Glen and Martin sitting on the wall, playing their game 'crisis'. They had to make up stories about what was in the cars and trucks driving along the dual carriageway which snaked up the valley below them.

'You see that red truck on its way down,' Glen was saying.

Martin scanned the vehicles shining under a chain of orange lights. He spotted the truck. 'Got it,' he said, 'big one with "Euro-Freight" written on the side?'

Glen nodded. 'That's got the zombies in it. That's where they've gone. They're all in the back of that truck and they're going off on a mission. They're going to wreak destruction on the first city they come to.'

Glen and Martin weren't surprised when Arwel came to join them.

'The zombies've gone,' he said.

'We know,' said Glen. 'The forest is dead. They went loopy after the Aberscary game. They went nuts. I was scared they were going to mash us.'

'You can't control zombies,' said Martin. 'They're not really human and they're capable of anything. I think they're on a bender.'

The three of them watched as the truck disappeared from view.

'Bet you wish you were in a lorry being transported to some place nobody can find you,' said Martin.

Arwel nodded.

'Don't worry about it,' said Glen. 'We'd be there to unload you.'

Arwel smiled as Glen patted his back. That was one good thing about Glen: he never changed sides. He was a good mate.

'Maybe,' said Martin, thoughtfully, 'you're only any good playing with zombies. Shame we've lost 'em.'

Arwel made his excuses. All he wanted to do was to get away and forget it all.

*

He pulled his door key out of his pocket. He knew that inside the house his dad would be full-on with rugby enthusiasm.

Chapter 2

Arwel pushed open the front door and stepped into the hall. He could hear the thumping of the bass drum upstairs. Dad thought the drums were the best part of his new Buddhist religion. He was always trying new religions. He said that they helped him think positively. His family knew that he really had just one religion – rugby – to which he always stayed true.

Arwel walked quietly through the hall towards the kitchen, hoping that Mr Rugby wouldn't realise he was home.

'Arwel!' Dad must have been listening out for him in between the thumps. 'It's me. I'm doing some positive thinking. Come up here now.'

Arwel climbed the stairs. He pushed the door to the little bedroom where his father kept the drum kit.

'One bad game does not a loser make,' said Dad happily, as he tapped the bass drum with his foot.

Arwel sat on the floor and listened to the beat. 'Dad,' he said. 'I'm rubbish.'

'You're not rubbish. You're fantastic. I saw you with my own eyes: you were incredible, you and that ugly bunch of characters. Steve reckons you could play for Wales – and he should know 'cos he plays for Wales under-nineteens.'

Arwel shook his head: 'Today was gross.'

'I know,' smiled his dad. 'Edwards told Benbow and he just texted me. You just need to reconnect with the positive images, Arwel. Imagine yourself scoring tries. Close your eyes. Let your mind run free through the pitches of your dreams. Visualise yourself into a stream of success. I've sorted it: tomorrow night down at the club – you're playing outside half for Aberscary.'

'What!' shouted Arwel.

The idea of turning out for his dad's team, playing at number ten and messing the whole thing up again, filled Arwel with dread. It was worse than thinking about going to the dentist. At least the dentist's was private. This was going to be another public humiliation.

That night Arwel lay awake in bed: he was visualising well – but what he visualised was awful. Dad and his mate Benbow were standing on the touchline, hanging their heads as he picked himself up off the floor again – and again – and Gilligan was laughing at him as he slipped around in the mud.

*

Dad was as good as his word. He pulled some strings and persuaded the club committee to drop the outside half and substitute Arwel. None of the players liked this. They couldn't see why a kid should play in a man's team, and their opponents weren't happy either because they thought that it made them look stupid.

Arwel stood in the middle of the pitch surrounded by grown men glaring at him. From the touchline his dad shouted encouragement, but even Benbow could see that something was wrong. Arwel looked small. He seemed lost.

'I don't think your boy's happy,' whispered Benbow, as Arwel wiped the ball clean before kicking off.

'Nonsense,' said Dad. 'That boy's a rugby genius. We've seen him play with our own eyes.'

'I dunno,' said Benbow. 'Maybe what we saw wasn't really true. I mean, who were those boys he was playing with? They looked very weird to me.'

Arwel took a deep breath. Once again he held the ball high before the kick-off. He kicked the ball forwards but it was another miss. The ball bounced away from him for a few metres and stopped in the mud. He could hear the other players grumbling.

The game was even worse than the one against Aberlairy School. Arwel was crunched in tackles, he dropped the passes that came to him and his own passes fell short. After half an hour the Aberscary captain jogged over to the touchline. He interrupted Dad as he screamed at the referee to stop the opposing pack from jumping on his boy. 'Sorry,' he said. 'Arwel's had enough. He's embarrassing the team.'

With that, Arwel was substituted. He trudged back to the changing rooms alone. It was over. In two days he'd gone from hero back to zero.

Benbow watched his old friend carefully. In the clubhouse he could see the rest of the committee muttering their disappointment. He knew that they were really angry with Dad for forcing them to play his son at outside half. If he couldn't see the problem, Benbow could. The committee didn't mind so much about Arwel – everyone has a bad game – but they were seriously cheesed off with his dad. He'd arranged a game for the firsts, which they'd lost to a team of weirdos, and now he'd selected his own son. That was unconstitutional.

'Look,' said Benbow. 'Let it go. Stop pushing everyone to play Arwel: he's not ready.'

'No way,' said Dad. 'I told you – my boy's a genius.'

Benbow shook his grey head. Arwel was not a genius, not in his opinion, and Dad was heading for trouble if he believed that he was.

Chapter 3

For the next few days Arwel kept out of everybody's way. He didn't hang around with Glen and Martin. He snuck out of Aberscary Comprehensive School as fast as he could at the end of each day and he stayed in during the evenings. He watched the telly, he played on his Xbox, and he got on his sister's nerves. The only place he visited was the forest, at night, alone. He wandered through the pine trees, searching for any trace of the zombies. But the place was dead quiet. It was as if they had never been there.

On Thursday evening, Arwel was in the forest, on his own, looking for zombies once again. They were his only hope. He drifted amongst the trees, calling their names: 'Delme, Gryff, Number Two.'

But nothing came back except for the sound of the breeze in the pine needles.

Suddenly, there was a sharp crack, the noise of a twig snapping. Arwel spun around. The forest was dark. He guessed it was a fox padding through the trees, looking for mice. 'Delme, Gryff, Number Two,' he called sadly. 'Come in, Number Two.'

'Arwel!' someone shouted.

For an instant, Arwel believed that the zombies were back. A huge smile spread across his face.

'I thought I'd find you up here,' said Beth, emerging from behind a tree trunk, smiling broadly.

Arwel took a step back. Beth, the girl from the school library, was the last person he wanted to see. He'd been especially careful not to walk home from school past her house, not to hang around anywhere near the library and to get out of all of her lessons as fast as he possibly could. 'What are you doing here?' he asked.

'I could ask you the same thing,' said Beth, 'and why are you wandering around talking to yourself?'

'Don't want to talk to anybody else,' said Arwel, moving away from her.

'Why?' she asked, following him.

'Did you follow me here?' asked Arwel.

'Why would anybody want to follow you?' said Beth. 'You're depressing.'

Arwel walked on. 'Then why are you here?'

'Why are *you* here?'

'I asked first.'

'I asked second,' laughed Beth, her eyes sparkling.

Arwel stopped walking. 'I'm looking for the zombies. In case you didn't notice, we had a team of rugby-playing zombies in this forest and now they've completely disappeared. I'm trying to find them.'

'Well that makes two of us,' said Beth, 'although I suspect I've got a little bit further in tracking them down than you.'

Arwel's face lit up. 'You know where they are?'

'Not exactly,' said Beth, 'but I do know something. Whilst you've been losing games and wandering around the place like a poet with a problem, I've been working at it.'

'Oh,' said Arwel, resuming his slow walk through the trees.

'Is that it?' asked Beth. '*Oh.*'

'Look, Beth. You don't have to pretend. I know everybody thinks I'm a loser. I think I'm a loser.'

'This isn't just about you,' said Beth.

'Isn't it?' said Arwel, looking very sorry for himself. He thought it was very much about him. He felt like the biggest idiot in Aberscary.

'Dur – it's about zombies, Arwel. There are fourteen half-crazed zombies charging around Wales at the moment and all you can do is feel sorry for yourself because you didn't play well in your last two games. Have you any idea how totally self-centred that is?'

Arwel thought for a minute. He shrugged.

'Things are happening, Arwel, and you're standing in a forest talking to yourself – how pathetic is that? We've got to find them. Have you seen the news? Have you read the papers? Have you been online?'

Arwel tried to say that he had been looking for the zombies, that it wasn't his fault that he couldn't find them. Beth grabbed him by the shoulders and shook him. 'I've been researching on the internet and in the library. Zombies can be dangerous, you know that.

20

Look at this.' She produced a newspaper cutting from her pocket and handed it to Arwel.

'*Mysterious Creatures Terrorise City Centre*'. The newspaper report described a wild group of zombie-like creatures on the rampage in Cardiff, scaring shoppers, frightening bus drivers. '*Something must be done*,' it said at the end of the article.

Arwel looked at Beth.

'And this . . . and this . . . and this,' she said, pulling out more newspaper cuttings. 'They've been all over the place: harassing windsurfers in Tenby, swinging on the transporter bridge in Newport . . . Wherever they've been – Bangor, Treorchy, Llandudno – they've brought trouble. All these reports,' – she shook the cuttings in his face – 'are about zombies. Our zombies. Not good, Arwel. They're OK, most of the time. They're under control. But winning that game just tipped them over. They became what the experts call "exfrastic". People aren't safe – in Aberscary, or anywhere in Wales – and it's our fault. DO YOU GET IT?'

Arwel stared at Beth, his mouth open. He realised that whilst he'd been sitting at home feeling sorry for himself, Beth had got her head around the problem.

'Exfrastic means a trance-like condition zombies experience when they go wild. Winning that game was so exciting it flipped them from being reasonably friendly, if a bit whiffy, to being totally off the scale. We've got to get them back and it won't be easy.

According to my research, an exfrastic zombie is one of the seven most dangerous things in the unknown world.'

'What are the others?' asked Arwel.

'Nobody knows.'

Arwel began to walk briskly across the forest floor as Beth explained to him how difficult it was to catch exfrastic zombies. He stopped at an old wheelie bin. 'We've got this,' he said.

'What is it?' asked Beth.

'It's a zombie trap.' Arwel explained how Glen and Martin had invented the zombie trap and then got themselves into trouble with the zombies. Though he'd thought it was a bit of a joke at first it had actually worked. Glen and Martin had attracted the zombies. Their only problem was that they didn't know what to do with them once they'd arrived.

Beth listened carefully. She wasn't quite convinced that an old wheelie bin would be enough to catch the zombies, but she didn't have any better ideas, and she knew that the zombies liked the forest. She and Arwel studied the bin. 'Of course,' she said, 'if it's a trap, it needs bait . . . human bait.'

'No problem,' said Arwel. 'Meet me up here before school tomorrow. I know someone who's made for the job. In fact he's an expert.'

Chapter 4

'Absolutely no way, no way, no way, no way, no way,' said Glen.

'Way, way, way,' said Arwel.

*

'Are you seriously telling me there's nothing to worry about?' said Glen, from the bottom of the wheelie bin.

'We're right behind you,' said Martin.

'We'll be hiding in the trees,' said Beth, clutching one of her files. Only last night there had been a report on *Wales Today* describing how an empty plane at the airport had been thrown, like a paper dart, from one end of the runway to the other. The studio experts were baffled. But Beth had made a note in her file – yet another zombie-related incident. Worryingly, she observed, the tricks the zombies were playing were getting wilder and more violent.

'You just sit in the wheelie bin, and as soon as a zombie comes along, we'll bang the lid on, turn the bin on its side and sort the zombie out,' said Martin. 'Remember, Glen – you know no fear.'

Glen nodded. That much was true.

'OK,' said Arwel, as Glen clambered out of the bin, 'we'll come back here this evening, before it gets too dark. We'll bring everything we need so we can catch them on their way out.'

Glen nodded. As they headed towards Aberscary Comprehensive School he muttered to Martin. 'I'm not sure about this. What happens if they attack like last time?'

Martin smiled: 'Don't worry, mate. Remember, you don't have a subconscious mind. You don't care about stuff like that. You're not scared about the possibility of being menaced by supernatural beings – to you it's just nonsense.'

Glen nodded. 'Yeah, I'm not scared. I don't get scared. I don't know the meaning of scared.' He shivered involuntarily.

*

Later that day, during the dinner break, Arwel found himself in a place he'd almost forgotten – the library.

There were a few geeky kids poring over books and working on computers. Some of them recognised him. They waved and said hello. Arwel realised that they had no idea about his rugby disasters: to them he was just another kid who used the library computers. He smiled back. He'd almost missed the place, with its shelves of shabby books, its long clean desks and the smell of curry gently wafting in from the canteen extractor fan outside.

He sat at a computer and tapped in his passwords. He was surprised he could remember them. Then he began to search on the internet for information about zombies and how to calm them down. A message popped up onto his screen. *Arwel, what are you doing?*

Arwel looked around. He stared back at the screen. He didn't know what to say. Was the computer watching him? Were the zombies somehow on his case? Were they inside the computer? He typed carefully. 'Nothing!' Then he added another word, 'really'.

Almost instantly the machine messaged back: *I don't think that's true, do you?*

Arwel watched the screen in amazement. He tapped it with his hand, just to make sure it wasn't broken.

'Now, now,' said a voice behind him. 'Don't vandalise the equipment. Rugby boys and computers don't normally mix. If it doesn't do what you want – hit it.'

Arwel turned as Beth walked into view, laughing as she tapped the keys on her mobile phone. 'You got my message?'

'How did you do that?' asked Arwel.

'We've got a network here – all the computers are linked in – I just included my phone in the group. I can text anyone in this room and it comes up on the screen.'

'Cool,' said Arwel.

'It's easy. I'll show you some time.' Beth plonked one of her files on the desk next to the computer.

'What do you think I've been doing up here for the last couple of weeks? Here's the research on catching zombies. It's possible, but we've got to be careful.'

She pulled up a chair and began to flip through the pages in her file. 'You see, we'll need to control the zombies one by one, calm them down, a bit like pets. You know, talk slowly and firmly to them and give them rewards.'

'Like dog biscuits?' laughed Arwel. 'You're mad. They'll splatter us all over the forest.'

'The state they're in,' said Beth, 'is very similar to the one werewolves experience when there's a new moon. Zombies are like wolves and wolves are like dogs: we give them dog biscuits and pat them on the head.'

Arwel leafed through some of the pages. There were printouts and articles all talking about zombies and states of craziness. There were also a couple of articles about werewolves and dog training. He wasn't completely convinced, but he hadn't had any better ideas. 'I can get some dog food from my dad's mate,' he said.

Beth patted Arwel on the head. 'Good boy!'

Chapter 5

Arwel sat opposite his sister at the kitchen table, a packet of Welsh Cheddar open in front of him. Dad stood by the window, scratching his head, whilst Mum nervously poured a cup of tea.

'No way,' said Arwel, picking at the cheese.

'Way,' said Tania, 'definitely. I missed my birthday for that stupid game of rugby with your team of misfit weirdos and now I want to do this instead.'

Mum put a cup of tea in front of her daughter. 'It's very expensive.'

'And you're saying I'm not worth it?' said Tania. 'I get the picture: what Arwel wants he gets. What I want is "too expensive".'

'It was rugby,' said Dad, turning to face Tania. 'Rugby's different.'

'In case you didn't notice, Dad, I don't play rugby.'

'You go out with Steve. He plays rugby,' said Arwel.

'Steve wants to come too – we're going to stay in a posh hotel in Cardiff and we're going to see a show, and have dinner in an Italian restaurant.'

'Have we got any dog food?' asked Arwel.

Tania gave him a look. 'All of us together as a family, we're going to do something nice for once,' she insisted. 'Arwel ruined my birthday. I'm seventeen years old and, to be honest, I'm fed up with all my friends asking me why I never do anything nice for my birthday. Charlotte Colucci went to Miami for hers, Leena Mansoor had a night out in a stretch limousine and Nia Perkins-Williams got given a car. What did I get? Another touchline, another crummy birthday and another load of mud on my shoes.'

'Won't it cost a lot, Tania?' asked Mum. 'I'm working all day at the solicitor's as it is, and doing shifts at the pub.'

They all looked at Mum.

Dad scratched his head some more. 'We'll do it,' he said. 'I don't want Tania thinking she's not special. Tania, you're special. OK, what are we going to see?'

'Andrew Lloyd Webber,' said Tania.

'I gotta go,' said Arwel, leaving the table.

He slipped out of the house just as Benbow arrived with a bag full of shopping. He seemed agitated. He hurried in, barely glancing at Arwel as he brushed past him. Then he turned and grabbed Arwel's arm. 'Is your dad in?' he asked in a quiet, serious voice.

Arwel pointed to the kitchen. He didn't really want to hang around with Benbow because, inevitably, the subject of rugby would come up. Arwel never wanted to see another rugby ball. He'd come to terms with the fact that he wasn't very good and, at the age of thirteen, he'd retired from the human form of the game.

He eyed Benbow's shopping. 'Got any dog food in there?'

'Bouncer's favourite,' said Benbow, holding up a bag of biscuits.

'Can I have a lend?' asked Arwel.

Benbow raised an eyebrow and looked at him quizzically. Clearly the boy was falling apart at the seams. Benbow felt sorry for him. He handed the bag over. 'No problem, boy. I can easy get some more. You're not going to eat them, are you?'

'Thanks,' whispered Arwel, before taking the bag and hurrying off.

When he arrived outside Martin's, Beth was waiting for him. She was holding a bag of dog biscuits too. It was already starting to get dark and a cold wind funnelled down the valley. Arwel shivered slightly as Glen and Martin trudged up towards the forest. He turned and looked at the trees. The branches were moving. He shivered again. That cold wind chilling his bones was unmistakable: he knew that they were back. He looked up at the sky. The last rays of sunlight splashed over the tips of the pine trees. He felt almost good about feeling scared, as if he was about to meet an old friend.

Arwel led the way as they walked into the heart of the forest clutching bags of dog biscuits. They could all sense the same thing. It had changed – the place had become harsh, dank and cold. Arwel didn't say anything, but he wondered privately if they were doing the right thing, whether they'd ever make it back out again.

*

Down in Aberscary, on the path to the rugby club, Benbow and Dad were hurrying to a meeting. They spoke breathlessly.

'No confidence?' blurted Dad. 'What's that supposed to mean?'

'They are confident,' said Benbow. 'They're just not confident in you.'

'I'll give them "no confidence",' said Dad, his trainers stamping on the paving stones. 'I've been with this club, man and boy, for almost forty years.'

'They think that you're biased, that you've favoured Arwel in the selection process,' said Benbow, his brown shoes tapping on the ground as his short legs strained to keep up the pace.

'How can I be biased?' snorted Dad. 'Arwel's a brilliant prospect.'

Benbow sighed. He'd spent days trying to get his friend to see a picture he didn't want to look at. He knew the whole of the rugby club was against Arwel's selection. They thought it had brought disrepute on the club.

Dad and Benbow pushed open the door of the committee room and were confronted by a room full of scowling faces.

Chapter 6

Glen looked up from the bottom of the wheelie bin. He could just about see Arwel, Beth and Martin peering down at him in the gloom.

'Remember,' said Martin, 'you know no fear – your brain doesn't "do" fear.'

'Why do I feel scared then?' asked Glen, clearly terrified.

'Because you're going to meet wild zombies,' said Beth helpfully, 'but don't worry: we're going to do the talking.'

Glen shifted at the bottom of the bin. It was cold and wet down there. He didn't like it.

'OK, Glen,' said Arwel, 'we're going to leave you now. We'll be hiding in the trees, waiting. Good luck.'

Arwel, Martin and Beth took up their positions a few metres away. They crouched low, Beth clutching her zombie files, Martin lying flat on the ground. Arwel, from behind a big tree, kept his eyes on the bin. He'd been in the forest often enough to trust his own instinct. The night was cold and dark. Above the forest the moon shone like a silver ghost. He could sense the zombies. He knew that they were watching too, waiting for the right moment.

The four friends stayed in position for what seemed like hours. The forest grew darker. But no zombies appeared. Martin nudged Arwel's foot, and shrugged as if to say they were wasting their time. But Arwel wasn't moving.

Then Glen popped his head out of the bin. It must have been incredibly cold in there: his face looked blue. 'Hey, guys,' he said, although all he could see were trees, 'when can I get out?'

Arwel was just about to stand up and call the whole thing off when a figure stepped out of the gloom. 'Stay where you are, Glen,' hissed Arwel.

Tall, plastered in mud, half man, half skeleton, the figure lurched towards the bin. It was Delme. His face was drawn and grim. There was no hint of a smile or anything human in his expression.

More zombies appeared from the trees. They looked even worse than when Arwel first met them, if that were possible. Their decaying arms stuck out of their jerseys, their skin was slug-slimy and the smell of fungus made Arwel feel sick. He pushed Martin back, and Beth grabbed hold of his arm.

'Oh no,' cried Glen and disappeared down into the bin. From inside he shouted: 'Martin! I'm scared. Get me out of here. I've discovered my subconscious mind and it's really massive.'

Arwel held Beth back until all the zombies had stepped out from behind the trees.

As the zombies edged forward and surrounded the bin, Delme looked down into it. 'Get him,' he ordered.

Arwel jumped up. 'No!' he shouted.

The zombies turned, none of them seeming to recognise him. They began to laugh, in that peculiar way zombies have, like a clicking cackle, the sound of crabs on a fishmonger's slab.

'Get him first,' said Delme, raising a bony finger and pointing at Arwel.

Martin began to crawl backwards, away from the clearing. Slowly he slipped back into the forest. Beth reached for her file. With trembling fingers she began to leaf quickly through the pages. But try as she might, she couldn't find what she needed.

'It's me,' said Arwel, holding up some dog biscuits. 'Calm down.'

Delme pointed his solitary eye at him. It wobbled in its socket. 'It's time for you to join us,' he hissed.

'Wait,' cried Arwel. 'It's me, Delme. How's it going?'

Two snarling zombies seized Arwel, whilst another grabbed a large stick with a sharpened point.

Beth stood up as if she knew what to do. 'If you do anything to Arwel you'll be zombies for ever!'

The zombies laughed. 'We're lost and gone already,' said Delme.

'But Arwel's your captain – he's the only one who can help you to win an international.'

Delme leant against the bin.

Glen stuck his head over the top to see what was going on.

'You promised that before, but nothing happened,' said Delme.

Two more zombies grabbed Beth. Glen screamed as they swung the stick towards her. Arwel tried to wriggle free but he couldn't break his captors' grip. Their grey hands were like cold slimy rocks. He watched in horror as Beth struggled. He could see the terror in her eyes: she wasn't thinking any more. 'Dog biscuits!' he yelled.

For a split second Beth looked confused. Her eyes flashed at Arwel as if asking him how he could talk about biscuits when she was on the point of being skewered by crazed zombies.

Arwel met her gaze and suddenly she remembered. Instead of struggling, she lifted up her free hand and patted one of the zombies on the head. 'There's a good boy,' she stammered, trying to suppress the fear in her voice.

The zombie shook his head and snarled, but Beth patted it again. 'Good boy,' she said, as the other zombies gathered around her.

This time the zombie didn't shriek or shout. Slowly he lowered his head. She patted it some more. Her hand made a soft splatting sound as it touched the slimy grey skin. It was like patting a fish. The zombie moved its head sideways, as a dog might. Clearly it liked the sensation.

The other zombies scowled.

'Good boy, there's a good boy,' said Beth,

growing in confidence. Carefully she reached for a biscuit from the bag in her hand. She handed one to the zombie.

The arms around Arwel slackened. Quickly he copied Beth, patting his zombies and offering them biscuits from his own bag. 'Good zombies,' he said. 'There, have one of these. Good boys.'

Slowly the zombies began to calm down, even Delme. Glen pulled himself out of the wheelie bin and began to give out his biscuits. Martin made his way back through the trees to see what was going on. He hid behind a clump of ferns and watched in amazement as the zombies began sitting on the floor to enjoy their feast whilst Arwel, Glen and Beth went around handing out more biscuits. One of the zombies made a joke. Someone laughed.

Delme joined in the laughter, chomping on a biscuit and nodding appreciatively. 'Great biscuits,' he said to Arwel. 'How did you know we liked 'em?'

'Well – Beth knew.'

Beth sat on the ground and explained how she'd realised that the excitement of winning the match might have affected them. Delme nodded and admitted that the zombies had spent the last few weeks rampaging through the countryside. 'We get like that,' he said. 'We can be bad news.'

Now that the zombies were normal again Arwel was really pleased to see them. So was Glen. Martin left his hiding place and came striding into the open.

'Hey, guys,' he said. 'Great to see you. Remember me? I'm your manager.'

Arwel reminded the zombies that their first game had just been a step towards the international match that would free them forever from their terrible curse.

'We'll get you a game,' said Matin. 'You'll beat a bigger team than Aberscary and then you'll do it. You'll get that international.'

But as they talked about the possibility of another game, a sad look crossed Delme's face.

'What's the matter?' said Arwel sharply.

'I don't quite know how to say this,' said Delme, 'but I don't think we'll ever play again. Something's happened. We've got a problem.'

Beth stopped handing out the biscuits.

'What?' they all asked.

'Have you counted us?' said Delme.

Arwel counted the zombies: there were just thirteen of them.

'You've lost one,' said Beth.

Delme nodded. 'It's Number Two. He's not here.'

'We can find him,' said Arwel. 'Can't we?'

Martin and Glen nodded slowly.

But Delme shook his head. 'If it's too hard for us zombies to find him, what chance have you got?'

Some of the zombies hung their heads in shame.

'You can't have lost him,' said Arwel.

Delme took a deep breath. 'It's worse than that. I

think he's been taken. Show them,' he said, turning to Gryff Griffiths, the Flying Wing.

Sadly Gryff pulled some branches off what looked like a pile of wood. He brushed the needles and twigs away with his arm until something bright appeared.

'Wow,' said Glen as Gryff cleared away more branches.

'It's a Lamborghini Gallardo,' said Gryff when he'd finished.

Arwel had never seen such a beautiful machine. It looked strange, too sleek and smooth for the rough dark forest.

'I really want one of those,' muttered Martin.

Delme explained what had happened. 'After the Aberscary game,' he said, 'we felt fantastic. We rushed out of the forest – we ran over hills and valleys – we went all over the place. We get like that.

'One night, we went to the big stadium. We scaled the sides like spider-men and looked down from the roof at the grass and the posts below. It was fantastic. I remember saying to the boys that one day we would get on that pitch and win our international. Then we dropped down from the roof and stood on the turf, getting a feel for the place. I remember looking around me at the seventy thousand empty seats, dreaming that one day we would be there in front of a cheering crowd. But then something happened.'

'I'd gone outside the ground,' said Gryff, '. . . and found the Lamborghini . . .'

'That's when Number Two was captured,' sighed Delme. The rest of the zombies had been running around on the pitch like in the old days. Delme thought that he might have seen a figure sitting high in the stands watching them, but he wasn't sure. Others thought they'd seen a shadowy man standing on the touchline. Afterwards, some of the zombies said that, perhaps, they'd seen someone talking to Number Two. Some said they'd seen him being led from the pitch, his head bowed, almost as if he'd been sent off.

The only thing they knew for certain was that Number Two had disappeared. They searched the ground but they found nothing, apart from Gryff and the Lamborghini.

'Who would want to take Number Two?' Delme asked.

Arwel, Beth, Glen and Martin listened to the story carefully. 'Perhaps he just got too excited by being in the stadium and went off exploring,' Martin suggested.

'No,' said Delme. 'That figure in the stands. Too much of a coincidence. Number Two was definitely taken.'

Arwel said nothing but he realised that the zombies were scared. He looked at their faces as Delme spoke quietly about the missing hooker and saw how worried they were. He thought to himself that if anything could frighten Delme, it had to be bad – very bad.

Chapter 7

Arwel skidded around the corner into Disaster Street. He was late. He unlocked the front door and tiptoed inside. He was expecting everyone to be asleep. Instead, the house shook with crashing and hammering. Dad was smashing the drums as hard as he could. Arwel rushed upstairs to find out what was happening but Mum barred his way to the drum room. She stood on the landing in her nightie, biting her nails.

'What's going on?' shouted Arwel over the crash of snares and cymbals.

'Your dad's been sacked from the committee,' said Mum. She looked tired and worried. She didn't even ask Arwel where he'd been. He made his way across the landing as Tania shouted from her bedroom, 'Make Dad be quiet, will you?'

But there was nothing anyone could do. In the end they went to their separate rooms to try to sleep through the racket. Even with the drumming pounding in his ears, Arwel couldn't think about his dad's problems. It didn't occur to him that perhaps he was the reason his dad had been sacked from the committee. He couldn't get Delme's story out of his head: it made his dad's worries seem lightweight in comparison.

All night Arwel thought about Number Two. Someone or something didn't want the zombies to play rugby.

*

As he hurried through the school gates the following day Arwel could see the teachers pulling up in the car park. Some of them watched him, almost warily, before bustling in, laden with bags and briefcases, scurrying towards the staff room – Arwel was early.

Inside the main building he strode purposefully down the long corridor, past the language laboratories and towards the changing rooms. He sat down on a bench and waited under the noticeboard. After ten minutes he spotted a figure in a green tracksuit bounding towards him. It was Mr Edwards. He bounced a basketball on the wooden floor as he approached.

'Good morning, Arwel,' he said. 'Come to apologise?' He smiled. 'Don't worry, boy. All players go through terrible periods when they can't even kick a ball straight. It happened to me,' he said, almost proudly. 'Players lose their nerve, they eat too much, they take up ballroom dancing – rugby is a one-hundred-per-cent lifetime of commitment. You'll bounce back.'

As if to emphasise the point he dropped the ball on the floor. 'See,' he said. 'Everything bounces back.'

Arwel didn't want to talk about his rugby career

but Mr Edwards had other plans. 'Now this may sound hard, Arwel, but it's fair. That's my way. You can't play for the firsts, or the seconds, or the thirds. But you can come training. You need to build up your confidence. Your commitment is one-hundred-and-ten per cent – no it's more, it's two-hundred-and-ten per cent – but your skills are close to zero. I'd even say that they're registering on the minus scale at the moment. Do you understand?'

Arwel nodded miserably.

'You know what a minus skill-level is?' said Mr Edwards, as he unlocked the door to his 'office', the little room between the changing rooms and the gym.

Arwel shook his head.

'It's the point where a player's presence on the field of play gives points to the opposition. It's when one of our team actually makes all the rest of the boys play worse. A player like you, on present form, would cost us about twenty points. I'm afraid we haven't really got that kind of buffer. Do you know what I'm saying?'

He threw the basketball at Arwel. Arwel caught it as Mr Edwards looked at his timetable. 'Good catch,' he muttered as he read.

'I've got a question about the rules of rugby,' said Arwel.

Mr Edwards looked up from his paper. His eyes gleamed. 'The *laws* of rugby,' he corrected, reaching for a well-thumbed manual on top of his cupboard. 'This, Arwel, is the rugby bible. If you've a problem you can always guarantee that the answer is to be found in here. He grinned as he thumbed the familiar pages. 'You're not thinking about becoming a ref? You don't have to be any good at playing to be a ref. You've just got to be smart. You're smart – when do you want to start?'

Arwel didn't want to be a referee. 'I've just got a question about replacement hookers.'

'Laws 3.5 and 3.13. Fire away,' said Mr Edwards happily, sitting with his feet plonked on his desk and pushing his chair so that it balanced on its back legs.

'What happens if you've got a team of fifteen players and you lose your hooker?' asked Arwel.

'Easy,' said Mr Edwards, almost disappointed. 'You can't play. The three members of the front row, the two props and the hooker, can only be replaced with "suitably trained and experienced players".'

'So if you haven't got a suitably trained and experienced hooker, a number two, you can't play?'

'Well, if it was a friendly you could do uncontested scrums, but it's hardly ideal.'

'What about an international?' asked Arwel.

'Forget it,' said Mr Edwards. 'Basically, without a hooker you can't play rugby.'

Arwel nodded, said thank you, and hurried back down the corridor, leaving Mr Edwards engrossed in the laws of rugby.

When Arwel caught up with Glen and Martin they were full of zombie talk. They wanted to go back to the forest, to organise matches, and drive the Lamborghini. But Arwel wasn't convinced. He'd put enough pieces together to understand that without Number Two there was no chance of the zombies playing and that that was the real reason why they were so mixed up.

Chapter 8

When Arwel arrived home that evening everything was in chaos. The front door was open and the house was full of people. Mum was making tea and Tania was sitting at the kitchen table, crying. Her boyfriend, Steve, stood behind her, looking serious. Benbow paced around in little circles near the kettle. His dog, Bouncer, sat next to a radiator. There was no sign of Dad.

'We didn't want to worry you, Arwel,' said Mum, 'but we can't find your dad.'

'He's disappeared,' said Benbow. 'It's the shock of being sacked from the committee.'

'I didn't sleep a wink,' wailed Tania, 'and now Dad's gone – completely. He's run off.'

Mum handed Arwel a cup of tea. She looked dreadful. She held up a little piece of paper. On it Dad had written 'Goodbye' in very bad handwriting. He'd signed it: 'Mr Rugby'.

'Of course,' said Tania, looking pointedly at Arwel, 'this is all your fault.'

Benbow nodded, adding quickly that it wasn't fair to blame Arwel.

'If you hadn't played so rubbish, Dad would still be on the committee and we'd still be going to Cardiff for the show,' Tania wailed.

'Don't be so selfish,' said Mum.

'Well, it's typical. Whenever I want to do something, he spoils it.' Tania pointed an accusing finger at Arwel.

Steve put his arm around her. 'Arwel can't help it – he's not very good. That's all there is to say about it.'

'I asked him not to pick me,' Arwel grumbled, 'but he didn't listen.'

'I've called the police,' said Mum. 'They're sending someone over. I know your dad, Arwel. He's done a runner. He's been up all night, working himself up into a frenzy of self-loathing.'

Benbow finished his tea. 'Right,' he said. 'I'm going to take a walk around all the places he likes going to.'

'Shouldn't take long,' said Arwel. 'The only place he likes is the rugby club and he's hardly going to be there.'

Benbow got up and walked briskly down the hall. Bouncer, rather reluctantly, followed him.

'Keep in touch,' shouted Mum.

Benbow held his mobile phone above his head.

The kitchen fell silent. Arwel shifted uneasily from foot to foot. Nobody told him not to worry. Nobody said it wasn't his fault. 'It's not my fault,' he shouted suddenly and ran out to the hall. Behind him he could hear his sister explaining why he was such a selfish weirdo.

Arwel drifted around the streets of Aberscary, half looking for his dad, half just trying to avoid going home. Eventually, as the street lights flickered into life, he found himself in Beth's road. He hurried up her drive and knocked on the door.

Beth's mum answered. She smiled and asked Arwel in. 'Beth's in the telly room. Would you like some biscuits?'

Arwel stepped into the warm house with its neat, deep carpets. He shook his head.

'I heard about your dad,' said Beth's mum, as Arwel walked down the hall. 'Mr Rugby got sacked from the committee and now he's gone missing. It's all over the town.'

'It's not my fault,' moaned Arwel.

'I know. How could it possibly be your fault?' She reached out and ruffled Arwel's hair.

Arwel found Beth on the sofa in front of her laptop. She glanced up at him. 'I thought you might come over,' she said. 'Bad news. But your dad probably hasn't gone far. I expect he's just walking up on the hills. You shouldn't worry too much.'

Arwel nodded numbly.

'You should be more worried about the guy who kidnapped Number Two,' she said. 'Zombies are quite straightforward creatures: cursed, half human. They're strong, but they're not...how can I put this...' She snapped her fingers as she tried to find a suitable word.

'Clever?' said Arwel. 'I never heard of a zombie with A-stars.'

Beth nodded but Arwel wasn't interested in what she had to say. He wished she'd stop talking. His dad was missing. He wanted her to help find him.

Beth was much more interested in the zombies. 'They're best in a team. On their own they just get a bit sad. Now, whoever it was that took Number Two has got to be pretty smart. I mean, if we didn't know the zombies so well, we'd have no chance trying to capture one. But this guy just turns up, spots Number Two and leads him away like a . . .'

'Like Benbow's dog,' said Arwel wearily. 'Where do you think my dad's gone?'

'Imagine being powerful enough to control a zombie like that,' continued Beth as if she hadn't heard him. 'I mean, Number Two is a front row forward – he's no pushover. Who or what would have that kind of power over him?'

Arwel tried to listen as Beth droned on about creatures from the underworld and who was in charge of who, but he couldn't concentrate and he kept thinking about his dad. He was sure he hadn't gone far, but he was also sure that being fired from the committee of the rugby club was about the worst thing that could happen to him. And in a way, it really was Arwel's fault. After all, he was the one who dropped the ball. He was the one who let Mr Rugby down.

Beth was still talking, trying to work out what kind of supernatural creature could control a powerful zombie like Number Two.

'I've got to go,' said Arwel suddenly.

'You're going to look for Number Two?' said Beth. 'Can I come?'

'No,' said Arwel. 'I'm tired of all this. I want to be on my own. I'm going to look for my dad.'

'I'll come too,' persisted Beth.

'No,' said Arwel, 'just leave me alone.' He stood up and hurried out as Beth's mum, smiling as ever, came in with a plate of biscuits.

Arwel walked past her and let himself out.

Chapter 9

Arwel didn't think he needed to join his family and Benbow scouring the streets and hillsides in search of his dad. But he didn't want to sit around talking about missing zombies either. Mr Rugby was in trouble and Arwel knew why. If he hadn't asked his dad to arrange that first game with the zombies he'd still be on the committee.

He wandered through the twilight, half looking, half thinking, heading where his feet took him. He found himself at the rugby club. The pitch was deserted. Arwel walked to the try line and stood under the posts, remembering the day he and his team of zombies beat Aberscary.

In the distance, past the floodlit stands, was the river. It was always dark down there. When Arwel was a kid his dad used to take him there fishing for eels.

He scrambled down the riverbank, making his way along a track through the brambles to the spot where they used to fish. It was half protected by an enormous tree root where they'd sit when it was sunny. Now it was hard to see. There were just the flecks of silver from the streetlights on the opposite bank. They glimmered on the wide, grey, gurgling river like the bellies of fishes.

Arwel looked again at the root. He saw a figure.

It looked like a garden gnome wrapped in a cloak of tree roots. It was staring into the black and silver water. There, in his favourite faded tracksuit, with his head in his hands, was Dad.

'Arwel, what are you doing here?' he said, brushing his hands across his face.

'Dunno,' said Arwel. 'Look, I'm sorry about the committee. I heard.'

'Most people in town have. I've been hiding down here to keep out of the way. I've got nothing to say.'

'Did they really sack you because of me?' said Arwel, sitting next to his dad on the bank.

'No,' said Dad, patting Arwel's head. 'They sacked me because I selected you.'

That didn't make Arwel feel so good.

'After forty years they booted me out just because of one bad game. It's very sad.'

'What would you say if I could get you back in?' said Arwel.

Dad looked across the pitch at the clubhouse. 'After what's happened, I wouldn't be interested.'

'Benbow, Hoof, all your mates are in that club. You can't just give up. You can't just walk away and hide down by the river,' said Arwel.

Dad looked at his son and smiled. 'Sometimes you have to recognise when you're beat, when it's someone else's turn to be Mr Rugby.'

'But you *are* Mr Rugby, the one and only, and I

can get you back on the committee. It's my fault they kicked you off,' said Arwel.

'You can't do anything. You've got no influence.'

'All right,' said Arwel. 'Be on a new committee. Be on my team's committee.'

Dad smiled, just to show Arwel he wasn't too depressed. He sighed and said, 'Hmm...'

'Good, now come with me,' said Arwel, leading his father away from the tree stump.

'Where are we going?'

'Our team's a man down and according to Laws 3.5 and 3.13 we're not allowed to play without a suitably trained and experienced hooker.'

'You're dead right, Arwel. Well done,' said Dad, 'but why don't we just replace him?'

'In this team you don't replace players – they play together or not at all,' said Arwel. 'We've got to find our hooker.'

A smile crossed Dad's face. He liked this idea. 'One for all and all for one, eh?' he said as they picked their way between the bramble bushes back up to the rugby ground.

'Hold it right there,' came a voice as a figure emerged from behind the corner of a bush.

Arwel gasped and his dad peered into the gloom. A small figure stepped out carrying a file under one arm.

'Beth! What are you doing here?'

'I followed you. Firstly you don't walk out of my

house without saying thank you to my mum for offering you biscuits and secondly you don't tell me to stop trying to help you find Number Two and then turn around and do it yourself. I'm coming with you.'

'There's no need,' said Arwel.

'I think there is,' said Beth. 'Your dad has no idea of the forces that he's up against and you've been so useless recently that there's a good chance you'll both end up being turned into zombies yourselves.'

Dad didn't understand. 'What are you talking about?'

'Nothing,' said Beth. She was determined. Her nose had reddened slightly in the cold air and her blue eyes flashed. She was angry.

'All right,' sighed Arwel. 'You can come with us.'

'Would you two mind explaining to me exactly what's going on?' said Dad. 'I'm depressed. I've run away from home.'

Beth spoke before Arwel could open his mouth. 'Very sorry about that, but there are some things that have to be kept secret. We can't tell you exactly what's up, but we can say that we've lost our hooker. Where would you hide a hooker?'

Dad thought as they picked their way back towards the ground. 'Well,' he said, 'not around here. When there's a game on we're always losing balls in the river. People come over here all the time trying to pull them out. Look.'

They could just make out the shapes of old rugby

balls trapped in the undergrowth on the opposite bank of the river.

'And I wouldn't keep him in town, because people would hear him trying to get out. Don't forget he's going to be very strong, so you'd need somewhere far away and really difficult to escape from. I'd keep him in a hole in the ground,' laughed Dad, 'a deep one.'

Arwel and Beth looked at him. 'Go on,' said Arwel.

'A hole in the ground,' Dad repeated, 'that's where I'd hide a big strong forward.'

Beth scrambled up the bank, trying to make notes in her file. 'I've got nothing on holes in the ground.'

'Sometimes,' said Dad, 'the answer isn't on the internet. You might just be standing on it. I've got a book at home. You can have a lend if you like.' Dad had cheered up. He hopped up the riverbank and onto the field. Arwel followed him.

'What's he mean?' Beth asked.

'Dunno,' said Arwel.

Chapter 10

When Dad and Arwel arrived home, it was to a huge sigh of relief. Mum hugged them both, and so did Tania. The policeman who had been called to look for a missing person shrugged his shoulders before finishing his tea and leaving. Arwel thought he seemed a little disappointed.

'Bye,' said the policeman. 'If anyone else vanishes, please don't hesitate to call.'

Then everybody started telling Dad off for disappearing so irresponsibly. He said he was sorry, that he wouldn't do it again. He promised not to play the drums. He announced that, as the new (and only) committee man for the Zombies Rugby Football Team, he'd arrange a game for them that would put them on the map and really show the committee of Aberscary Rugby Club what they were missing.

Then he took Arwel up into the drum room.

'You're not allowed to play – no more primal beats,' said Arwel.

Dad looked at his son. 'I've got a feeling that missing hooker of yours is a bit special. You certainly need him. You can't play a game without him,' he said, taking a book off an empty shelf behind the drum kit. 'I don't read much, but this book might help. Have a look and see what you think. Benbow gave it to me.'

Arwel took the book. It was a paperback full of tightly packed print and old black-and-white photographs. The book was called *The History of Aberscary* by Carlos M. Benbow.

Arwel read the name of the author out loud.

'Benbow's dad,' said Dad with an air of respect. 'He was a clever man. If you need to know where in Aberscary you could hide a missing prop, this'll tell you.'

*

Even though there was no drumming that night neither Arwel nor his father slept. Dad was trying to work out which stadium would be best for the next zombie game. Arwel was reading *The History of Aberscary*.

Chapter 11

As they walked away from Aberscary Comprehensive at the end of the day, Arwel explained his plan to Glen, Martin and Beth. Martin and Glen weren't impressed. They'd spent the previous evening with the zombies in the forest.

'They were pathetic,' said Martin. 'They wouldn't scare a mouse.'

'I preferred them when they were crazy,' said Glen. 'Depressed zombies aren't great fun to hang around with. They just wander about the forest grumbling. They wouldn't even let me drive the Lambo.'

'That's why we're going to find Number Two,' said Arwel. 'We're going to put the team back together.'

'Where,' asked Beth, 'are we going to look?'

'A hole in the ground. Where better to hide a zombie?'

'What, like in a drain?' said Glen.

Arwel didn't speak. He just marched on and the others followed. They hurried past the rugby ground, past Neil Kinnock Avenue and the new houses leading down to the main road and out along the lanes into the countryside. They kept going until they came to some metal railings and a big fence with a rusty sign on it. 'Private Property – Keep Out'.

'What's this?' asked Martin. 'I've never noticed it before.'

'Nor me,' said Arwel, 'but I do know this. There's an old coal mine the other side of that fence. I read about it in this book Dad gave me. It hasn't been used for years.'

Beth smiled. 'You reckon this is what your dad meant when he said a hole in the ground would be a good hiding place?' she asked.

'Biggest hole I could think of,' said Arwel. 'If I wanted to hide a fifteen-stone front row forward I'd look for somewhere very deep and very difficult to get out of.'

'But there must be hundreds of old mines around here,' said Martin. 'What's so special about this one?'

'Most of them are filled in,' said Arwel. 'This is the only one round here that isn't.'

'Why not?' asked Glen.

'According to Carlos M. Benbow they were preserving it. It had an unusual reputation for being the only mine never to have a problem with gas.'

'Not like Glen, then,' laughed Martin.

Arwel took no notice. 'They started to preserve it, but then they ran out of money and now it's just kind of forgotten about,' he said, searching along the fence for a way in. Eventually he found a broken railing, squeezed through the gap and led the way towards a cluster of buildings half covered in ivy.

'Come on, Glen,' said Arwel. 'Push!'

'It's all right for you – you're smaller than me. And I can't see.'

The light was starting to fade, so Arwel put his torch on. Bats flitted low over their heads. Martin ducked and made a funny little scream. Glen and Beth laughed.

'You're not frightened again?' giggled Beth.

'I'm not,' stammered Martin.

'You ran away when the zombies came,' said Glen.

'It was a tactical manoeuvre,' said Martin.

Arwel pointed his torch at a building. Above it was an old sign. 'Pithead'.

'I think this is it,' he said.

They pushed their way past the rotting door and into a room about the size of a classroom. The walls were made of bricks, it was damp and there were pools of water on the concrete floor. They looked up and saw grey-pink clouds catching the last rays of sunlight through the gaps in the roof.

'Are you seriously telling me Number Two is in here?' said Martin.

'No,' said Arwel, flashing his torch at the side wall of the room. 'He's down there.' A huge stone archway, like the entrance to a railway tunnel, was cut into the side of the valley. Carved into the stones of the archway were the words 'Eight Miles Down'.

'It's a coal mine,' he whispered. 'It's called Eight Miles Down.'

'Awesome,' said Glen.

'I don't like the name,' said Martin.

They peered into the tunnel. Even with the torch it wasn't possible to see much.

'This is it,' said Arwel. 'Could you think of anywhere better for hiding a zombie?'

'I'll keep watch,' said Martin. 'You always...'

'...need someone in reserve?' Beth finished his sentence.

*

Arwel, Glen and Beth stepped into the mine, their footsteps echoing deep in the mountain of rock. 'Number Two!' shouted Arwel, flashing his torch across the walls. His words bounced back in an echoing chorus. The tunnel was deep. Spiders and beetles skittered out of the glare, slithering into watery gaps.

Then there was silence.

They edged forward, trying to ignore the drips of cold water falling from the ancient roof. 'I suppose this place is safe,' said Glen as they moved deeper and deeper down into the tunnel.

Arwel laughed. 'Does it feel safe?'

'Not really,' said Glen.

'What does Carlos M. Benbow have to say?' whispered Beth.

'There were a couple of roof collapses,' said Arwel. 'Not that uncommon apparently. But it's not going to fall down today, is it? We'd have to be ridiculously unlucky for the roof to cave in on us right now.'

Some flecks of brickwork detached themselves and sploshed, menacingly, into a big puddle.

'NUMBER TWO!' Glen shouted. 'Get a move on. We gotta get out of this place quick.'

There was no answer. As they walked, their eyes grew more accustomed to the torchlight. They could see that the tunnel was quite wide and easily high enough for a man to stand up in. There were metal tracks running along the floor and occasionally they'd pass an old coal waggon left rusting on the side of the tunnel.

'Look at that,' said Beth. The tunnel widened for a few metres and Arwel flashed his light over a group of what looked like wooden stalls, with water troughs and discarded feed sacks. There was even an old halter.

'They used horses to pull the trams,' said Arwel. 'When they came out, most of the ponies were blind. That was in *The History of Aberscary* too.'

'This place gives me the creeps,' said Glen.

There was a shout from Martin, guarding the entrance. His words bounced down the tunnel. 'Are you lot OK?'

'Yes!' they shouted.

From out of the gloom hissed a different voice: 'That's a matter of opinion.'

Arwel swung his torch around. Glen grabbed his arm and Arwel grabbed Beth's arm.

'You're about as far from OK as you are from the entrance of this mine,' said the voice. It sounded like slime slipping over stone.

'Where are you? Who are you? What are you?' asked Arwel, swinging the torch beam wildly around the tunnel.

'Get out of my mine,' said the voice. 'There's work going on here.'

'Work?' said Beth. 'What sort of work?'

'I think you'll find that mining operations ceased at the Eight Miles Down pit more than fifty years ago,' said Arwel.

'Did you swallow that book?' whispered Glen.

They could hear the hiss of steam and the clank of metal: something was rolling towards them along the old track running through the middle of the shaft. Arwel shone his torch into the gloom. 'We just wondered,' he said, edging forwards, 'whether you might have seen a lost zombie?'

They could see the shape now. It was black, riding on steel wheels – an old steam engine, covered in rust, soot and oil. At the back, bathed in orange light from the fire beneath the boiler, they saw a thin shadowy figure wearing a hard black hat. He was leaning out towards them. His face was white as bone and his eyes were sunk into his skull as if he hadn't slept for years. 'Get out of here, and don't come back!'

'I think we should just do what the man says and

get out,' said Glen. 'Sorry to bother you,' he added cheerfully. 'We were just passing. See you.'

But Arwel stood firm. 'His name is Number Two.'

Beth tried to pull him away.

'Strong as an ox? Never shows up to work?' said the man as he pulled a lever and brought the strange engine to a hissing stop. It was almost close enough to touch, oil dripping down its sides, and steam fizzing from its joints.

Arwel gulped. He nodded.

'Maybe I've come across him,' said the man in the cab.

'He's a zombie,' said Beth helpfully. 'We don't know anything about his work habits.'

'He owes me time,' said the man. 'Let me assure you, before he was a zombie, your man never turned up for work on time. He was one-hundred-per-cent late and one-hundred-and-ten-per-cent idle. I was in charge of his team of colliers. Nobody misses my shifts and gets away with it. You follow the direction of my argument?'

Arwel's torch flashed onto Glen's face. It was white with fear.

'Are you saying you're keeping Number Two here because he was down on his flexi?' said Beth. Her mum worked for the council – she was always going on about making up her hours so that she could take a day off.

'He's got a lot of digging to do,' laughed the man

as he shovelled some coal into the engine's boiler. 'He's going to dig and dig forever. To make up for all that lost time.'

'It's like being given a detention,' muttered Glen. 'They get you in the end.'

Arwel took a deep breath. 'We just want to find Number Two, so he can come and play for us.'

'Miners who don't turn up to work, who skive off to play rugby, who don't produce the required amount of coal, they have to pay back their hours some time or other. That's my job – they call me the Overman – I make sure that every man works his share. He's been missing from work for one hundred years. To make that lot up he owes me precisely 36,500 days of toil.'

'There's 365 days in a year,' said Beth, who felt that Glen needed some help. 'A hundred years times 365 equals 36,500 days of work.'

'I knew that,' said Glen, scratching his head.

The Overman held out his arm and pointed with his pickaxe. Arwel followed with his torch beam. 'Is that Number Two?' he stammered.

Deeper in the mine, crouching with his back bent, a lonely figure lifted his pick and brought it crashing down. He turned, covering his eyes as if blinded by Arwel's light. Number Two swung his pickaxe again, clattering it into the wall of coal.

'Poor Number Two,' whispered Beth.

The zombie groaned and swung his axe.

'A hundred years ago this man played rugby,' said

the Overman. 'And he played me for a fool. Now he's paying his debts.' He pulled another lever and the engine hissed as a great iron crane lifted and extended towards Arwel. The Overman's hands flew across the controls. With a great roar of steam, a huge iron pipe rose slowly from the side of the engine and pointed menacingly.

The Overman glared gleefully at his visitors.

Arwel, Beth and Glen pulled back, pressing themselves into the slimy walls of the tunnel.

'Now,' said the Overman. 'You never worked for me, but if you come back here, I'll get some hard graft out of you too. You're old enough to push coal. I'll keep you down here until you're scared of the daylight.'

'But...' said Beth. She was about to argue.

'Time for some steam,' the Overman cried, linking his grey hands around a lever and pulling hard. The engine blared and flames poured out of its chimney. He roared with laughter. 'Fire!'

Flames began to shoot out of the iron pipe as the massive crane began to sweep from side to side. It just missed Glen.

'That thing's going to shoot us!' shouted Arwel, turning in the direction of the mine entrance. 'Run!'

From far away in the distance they could hear Martin's reply. 'Already running!'

Chapter 12

In the kitchen, Mum and Dad were gazing at Tania and Steve. Tania wore a long blue silky dress. Steve was wearing a black jacket, black trousers, a white bow tie and a white shirt.

'I think you both look beautiful,' Mum was saying.

'Really fabulous,' said Dad, fingering his tracksuit bottoms.

Arwel hurried in, slightly breathless after his encounter at Eight Miles Down.

'What do you think, Arwel?' asked Tania, turning around like a supermodel.

'Not a bad bit of kit, eh?' said Steve, puffing out his chest.

'Er, cool,' said Arwel.

'This is my prom dress. Mum thought it'd do for going to the show,' said Tania. 'I'm not sure though. I mean, it should be new, shouldn't it? What are you wearing, Arwel? We've got the tickets, the hotel's booked and we're going to a restaurant too. For once this family is going to do things properly.'

Arwel had forgotten about the trip to Cardiff. 'Oh, something smart,' he lied. 'I haven't decided yet. Does anybody know anything about Eight Miles Down?'

'What's Eight Miles Down?' asked Tania. 'Is it a nightclub?'

'It's a disused coal mine,' said Arwel. 'I just wondered if you'd come across it.'

Tania looked at Arwel in disgust: 'No I haven't, surprisingly. You know me, Arwel: I love to go looking around old coal mines.'

'We don't "do" coal mines,' explained Steve.

'It's no good,' said Tania, after some deliberation. 'I need new.'

'Tania's right,' said Dad. 'If we're going to see a show, we're going to need some decent clothes. I want something cool, you know what I mean? I can't go in my tracky and you, Arwel, look about as presentable as one of your rugby players. If I'm going to be the committee for your team, I've got to look the part. I've got to look like a man with a plan.'

Arwel couldn't help smiling. His dad wasn't exactly famous for his plans.

'Come on, Arwel,' said Dad. 'It's about time we bought you a suit. Down the retail park, yeah?'

'What?' The last place Arwel wanted to go was to Aberscary Retail Park for late-night shopping.

*

'You feeling better, Arwel?' asked Steve as they were getting into his Ford Fiesta.

For an instant Arwel didn't know what Steve was talking about, then he remembered the games of rugby he'd lost. Somehow, they seemed like ancient history.

'You're bouncing back?' asked Steve, clipping himself into the driver's seat.

'I suppose I am,' said Arwel, squeezing up next to his dad in the back.

'You want to play again?' asked Steve, as the others clambered in.

'Yes,' said Arwel, as Steve started the engine. 'I suppose I do.'

Dad couldn't hold back any longer. 'He's got a new management structure,' he said as the car bumped off down the street. 'Arwel and me – we've had a chat.'

As Steve drove, Tania, who was sitting in the front passenger seat – being in the back made her feel sick – said she was sorry that the committee had sacked her father. Mum was holding Dad's hand, Arwel couldn't help noticing. He was sitting between them in the back. Their hands met on his lap. He looked down at them. For a second he remembered the Overman's grey, bony hands. He shivered – the only creatures he'd ever seen with such creepy-looking hands were zombies.

'I'm going to be the committee for his team – the Zombies,' said Dad. 'We're going to be big – we're going to be bigger than big – we're going to be spectacularly big.'

Mum released his hand. 'Oh, so you're still interested in rugby?'

'More than ever,' said Dad. 'Never give up, never, never give up.'

'You gave up the other day,' said Mum almost hopefully.

'Arwel talked some sense into me.'

Arwel could feel his mum move a fraction of a centimetre away from him.

'I'm back to normal. I had a temporary blip. Now all I want is to make Arwel's team the best side in Wales,' said Dad, thumping the back of Tania's seat. 'As the Buddha says, or would say if he was interested in rugby, "giving up sucks".'

*

Steve's little Fiesta zoomed down the dual carriageway towards the retail park. On the hillside, sitting on the wall outside Martin's house, Glen and Martin watched the tiny vehicle. They didn't know who was in it. They were talking about the best way to spring Number Two from his prison at Eight Miles Down. Behind them, hidden by the shadows of the trees, stood thirteen zombies. They were watching the car too, edging closer and closer to the wall, trying to catch the drift of the boys' conversation.

*

Arwel wandered uncomfortably through the racks of brightly lit clothes while Tania and Steve gazed at themselves in mirrors as they tried on an assortment of shirts, dresses, shoes and jackets. Arwel's mother bought herself a neat black suit which she said would be economical because she could wear it for work afterwards and even behind the bar in her sister's pub. Steve and Tania bought new outfits to replace their old prom clothes.

They made Arwel buy a suit. He hated it. It felt just like school uniform. Everybody said he looked really old and smart, and this made him feel even worse. Dad chose a black dinner jacket, a purple shirt with frills down the front and a black bow tie. He insisted on wearing it out of the shop. 'This is the business,' he said. 'Now I look like a real mover and shaker. Tomorrow I'm going to start moving and shaking.'

On the way home everybody was happy, apart from Mum and Arwel. Arwel wasn't happy because he thought he looked like a creep and Mum wasn't happy because she knew that they could not afford all those new clothes.

When Arwel finally got to his room he was tired. But he didn't sleep. He started to read more from *The History of Aberscary* by Carlos M. Benbow.

Chapter 13

Arwel stumbled into the kitchen for breakfast the next day, yawning. His dad bounded past him as he hurried towards the front door, mobile phone in one hand, a snatched piece of toast in the other. Arwel was just about to say good morning when his dad interrupted him. 'Laters, Arwel,' he said, holding the piece of toast in front of his face. 'Got to leverage myself some face time with the big cheeses. Talk to the toast.' Then he disappeared into the street, walking briskly towards the bus stop.

Arwel thought that his dad's enthusiasm for the next game was good, but it wasn't useful. He knew that the Zombies didn't have enough players and that the team's outside half couldn't catch, kick or pass a ball. He thought the best thing to do would be to arrange some training sessions, so that he and his team mates could build confidence and fitness whilst they worked out how to free Number Two from Eight Miles Down.

When Arwel arrived in school he searched for Glen and Martin to tell them to get ready for intensive training but they weren't around. He tried all the usual places – the basketball hoop, the changing rooms – in the end he went to the library to see if Beth knew where they were.

She was working at a computer. When he asked her about Glen and Martin she just shrugged and shook her head. She was busy making another file to collect all the information she could about Eight Miles Down. 'The funny thing is,' she said as she pointed to the computer screen, 'according to all the maps there's no such place as Eight Miles Down. Look – it's not even on *Google Earth*.'

Arwel followed Beth's finger along Neil Kinnock Avenue, through the lanes to the place they had been – but according to the screen it was just trees. Even when they used the satellite picture where they'd found the coal mine, all the screen showed was a green patch.

'They do that sometimes,' said Beth.

'Who?' asked Arwel.

'The map people, the people in charge, when they want to hide something like an alien landing point or a secret army place. They just put trees on it. So the enemy can't find it.' She turned to face Arwel. 'You know what that means?'

Arwel shook his head slowly. He hadn't a clue what it meant.

'They know about the Overman,' said Beth. 'He's real, so real they've taken him off the map.'

Arwel nodded. 'Who's "they"?'

'I dunno: the council, the government maybe. He's such a threat to society that they'd rather keep him away from the general public – that is serious.'

'I know it's serious,' said Arwel. 'He's stolen our Number Two.'

'It's worse than that, Arwel. If the map people know and the government knows, then this is a supernatural secret.'

The bell for registration clanged, causing Arwel to jump slightly. Beth logged off the computer. As they were leaving the library, she asked: 'Where did you say Glen and Martin were?'

'That's what I'm asking you?' said Arwel. 'I can't find them.'

After school Arwel went straight to Beth's. Her mother smiled at him and offered him a plate of biscuits.

'Yes please,' he said, and then he added, 'I'm sorry about the other time.'

'What other time?'

Beth came bounding down the stairs. She'd changed out of her uniform and was wearing jeans, a pair of trainers and a big coat. 'We'll take the biscuits with us,' she said, grabbing one.

'No tea?' asked her mum.

'Thank you very much, for everything,' said Arwel as he carefully and solemnly shook her hand.

As they walked back to the road Beth told Arwel that now he was possibly overdoing the politeness thing. 'Mum'll think you're nuts.'

First they went to Glen's. He lived in a terraced house not far from Arwel in Galaxy Street. He lived with his mum and his two younger brothers, Alfie and Ryan. They were not much more than babies and most of the time they ran around in just their pants. Glen never bothered with them. His mum was so busy with Alfie and Ryan that she didn't really bother with Glen either. He fixed his own breakfast and was allowed to come and go pretty much as he pleased, so long as his mum knew where he was.

'Is Glen in?' asked Arwel, standing on the doorstep.

Glen's mum smiled. She pushed her grey-blonde hair out of her eyes. Behind her, Arwel could see Alfie and Ryan.

'Hiya.'

They both waved back. 'Hiya, Arwel,' they chorused.

'Sleepover,' said Glen's mum. 'He's up at Martin's. Didn't you see him in school today?'

Beth was just about to say that Glen hadn't been in school when Arwel nudged her sharply. 'Oh yeah,' he said. 'We just wanted to go for a kick around.'

Glen's mum smiled. 'Here,' she said, 'you two look cold – we're just having tea. Want a biscuit?'

Arwel and Beth thanked her and set off for Martin's.

Martin's house was on its own, a big old house on the side of the hill. It was the last house before the forest. It was always colder and wetter up there than down in the town. Arwel and Beth shivered as they rang the doorbell. Martin's older sister answered the door. She held a bottle of nail polish in one hand

and a brush in the other. She looked cross with them for interrupting her. They explained that they were looking for Martin.

'Martin?' she said. 'He's down at Glen's. Sleepover.'

Arwel nodded, almost as if he was expecting it.

They made straight for the forest. Immediately Beth started talking about the boys' disappearance. She was sure that it had something to do with the mysterious mine, Eight Miles Down. 'They shouldn't be allowed out on their own. They've done something really dumb. I know it,' she said, as they reached the first pine trees.

Arwel felt that she was almost pleased that they'd gone missing. 'OK,' he said. 'Keep quiet now.'

They walked in silence through the trees until they felt the chill in the air and smelt the strange toadstool smell of zombies.

'Look,' said Arwel. He pointed into the forest. There, between the trees, were the zombies, some lying flat on the ground, others on home-made beds of leaves and twigs. In amongst the injured were Martin and Glen, bandages on their heads and arms. Covered in dust and dirt, they lay on the ground, groaning and looking remarkably similar to their zombie friends.

'It's like *Casualty* for the un-dead,' said Arwel.

'What happened?' asked Beth, suddenly sounding really concerned. She rushed over to Glen and Martin.

Delme approached slowly. 'Arwel,' he said apologetically, 'we've made a mistake.'

Arwel sighed. He looked around at the devastated zombies. 'Big time, by the look of things. What have you done? What's happened?'

Delme looked embarrassed. 'We took matters into our own hands,' he said. 'We went to war without you.'

'I went on one late-night shopping trip,' exploded Arwel. 'I go away for one evening and look what happens.'

Beth, who was kneeling by Glen and Martin, glanced up at Arwel. He could see the look of worry on her face.

'We're sorry,' they moaned, holding their heads. 'We won't do it again.'

'That's the first and last time I listen to you boys,' said Delme. 'Their idea was to attack the Eight Miles Down mine.'

'Attack?' asked Beth.

'Full-frontal-straight-through-the-mineshaft attack, fifteen of us, all armed with sticks and stuff. We drive in shouting and screaming as loud as we can. We advance into the dark past the stables until we reach Number Two. We create a defensive formation around him, and Martin and Glen saw off his chains, using hacksaws. We hold back the Overman and his machines. When Number Two is free we just run out of the mine.'

'What?' said Arwel.

'A straightforward plan,' continued Delme. 'All of my zombies could understand it.'

'Who thought of it?' asked Beth.

Arwel thought this was a very silly question. It was patently obvious to him whose plan it was.

'Me,' said Glen, sitting up.

'Glen,' said Martin from the next bed. 'You don't do plans – not in future. You just do fearless.'

'You've got to admit we were fearless,' said Glen. 'We were so fearless. We were awesome.'

'Speak for yourself,' said Martin. 'I've always got fear. And this time I was right. We all ran in, according to the plan. We shouted and screamed and we got halfway down the mine. We could even see Number Two. Then it all went wrong.'

'The Overman hit us with the lot,' said Delme. 'It was man against metal in there. We were lucky to get out in one piece.'

'He was expecting you,' said Beth. 'You walked straight into his trap.'

'But that wasn't the worst part,' said Gryff the Flying Wing from his makeshift bed.

'What happened?' asked Beth.

'We scrambled out as best we could,' said Gryff.

'We escaped, but we lost something,' said Delme, 'something vitally important.'

'It's all my fault,' said Glen. 'I never want to do another plan again.'

Gryff hopped up off the floor. 'Notice what's missing?'

'Oh no,' said Arwel.

'You've only got one leg,' said Beth.

'He can't play on the wing like that. It'll decrease his speed by fifty per cent. He'll be a sitting duck,' said Delme.

'It fell off underground,' said Gryff apologetically. 'I can fix it back on – but first we've got to find it.'

For the first time since he was a small boy, Arwel lost his temper. He didn't go mad and start shouting. He didn't curl up in a ball and cry. He didn't moan about the fact that the Overman had now taken precisely one and a half of their best players. Arwel just stared intently, first at Delme, then at Martin and finally at Glen.

They could all tell he wasn't happy with them.

'Martin,' said Arwel coldly. 'Why didn't you stop these idiots?'

Martin shook his head. 'Dunno,' he moaned. 'I was persuaded by arguments that seemed compelling at the time.'

'What were you thinking of, Delme?'

Delme hung his head.

'Listen up!' barked Arwel.

Everyone fell silent.

'Our next game of rugby is being arranged. If we win that, people will hear about us. They'll read about us in the newspapers, we'll be mentioned on the telly and they'll have us on the internet. We'll be one step closer to getting to play an international. If you guys want to stop being zombies, you have to win that game. But it takes a long time to build up a reputation. So don't expect miracles. The more people know about us, the more chance there is of getting our international. I'm fixing my side of the deal. We're going to play again. But this only works if we've got a team. From now on we do things my way. No more attacks. No more moaning. I want you out training every night and I want you two,' Arwel pointed at Glen and Martin, 'to get home right now.'

'It's OK,' said Martin. 'We texted our mums. They think we're having a sleepover. It's really clever – you see Glen's mum thinks I'm at Martin's and my mum thinks I'm at his.'

Arwel shrugged his shoulders. 'I'll see you all back here tomorrow night, training.'

'What about my leg?' asked Gryff.

'First we need to catch the ball, then we'll figure out how to run with it,' said Arwel before marching out of the forest.

Beth followed. 'What's the plan, Arwel?' she asked.

'I dunno,' said Arwel. 'I'll think of something. Do me a favour – stay with Glen and Martin and try and tidy them up. I'm going to practise my kicking down the park.'

In the background they could hear Delme organising what was left of the team. 'You heard Arwel. Get up! Get off the floor! Come on!'

Chapter 14

For the next few days everybody was busy. Dad spent a lot of time on the phone and started going out to meetings with his new contacts. Whenever anybody tried to talk to him he would simply hold up his hand and say: 'Talk to the hand or leave a message on my BlackBerry.'

Tania was happy: the tickets for the show had arrived and she and Steve drove around Aberscary telling all their friends. Mum was busy doing extra shifts at the pub to pay for all their new clothes and Arwel and the zombies began some serious training.

At school things were different. Glen and Martin had been grounded. When Martin arrived home wrapped in bandages his mum rang Glen's to ask what exactly had happened at the sleepover. It didn't take long to work out that the boys had lied to them – so Glen and Martin both had to stay in.

'Man, it's like torture,' said Glen in the school canteen as he dipped his chips in his gravy. 'Ryan and Alfie are on at me all the time – they're worse than those steam engines.'

'You've a lot in common with Ryan and Alfie,' said Martin.

'All they want to do is hit each other,' said Glen. 'I'm more sophisticated than that.'

Arwel had been quiet up until that point. 'We've got to work out a way of getting Number Two out of the mine,' he said.

Glen and Martin shook their heads. 'Sorry, Arwel,' said Martin, 'grounded is grounded. You'll have to do it on your own.'

Arwel nodded.

'How's the training?' said Martin.

'Good,' said Arwel.

Just then Gilligan barged into Arwel's back. 'Hey, look who it is, Mr Loser himself. Enjoying your meal?'

Arwel didn't take any notice.

'I hear your dad's trying to put a team together,' said Gilligan.

'So?'

'It's pathetic. He's as pathetic as you. He gets fired from Aberscary so all he can do is get some bunch of losers together and pretend that they're a team.'

As Arwel got to his feet, Gilligan jabbed the chair into the back of his knees, causing his legs to buckle. He fell to the canteen floor, followed, seconds later, by his food. Everybody turned around to look.

'See!' shouted Gilligan. 'He even drops his meatballs.'

Gilligan strutted off just as Miss Jenkins, the science teacher, wandered over to see what the fuss was about.

'It's Arwel,' said Gilligan. 'He's getting ideas above his station.'

Arwel clambered to his feet and brushed bits of meatball off his shirt.

'Try to eat a little more carefully in future,' said Miss Jenkins.

*

At the camp in the forest the zombies had got down to some serious training. They practised tackling by running at the pine trees, they jinked and sidestepped around the larches and they kicked rocks high into the air. But Arwel could tell that their hearts weren't in it. Gryff Griffiths had to stand on the side, on his one leg, whilst Delme and the others rushed around as fast as they could.

Sometimes Beth would come to watch them. They were looking quite good, their multi-coloured jerseys filling out as they grew stronger. But she had to admit there was something missing.

As they walked home from school one evening Arwel explained about the missing something. 'It's belief,' he said.

'What do you mean?' asked Beth.

'None of us really believes we can do it.'

'Do what?' asked Beth.

'Exactly,' said Arwel. 'We're training every night, we're practising moves, but we're pretending. We haven't got a game, and even if we did have a game, we couldn't play because we don't have a hooker. Our winger's only got one leg and I've lost my nerve.'

As they made their way through the steep terraces of Aberscary towards Disaster Street, Arwel told Beth how he'd overheard some of the zombies muttering about how hopeless everything was. How they were training for nothing. How they'd never win another game, never win another international and never stop being zombies. He told Beth that he suspected that they were about to give up.

Beth thought for a moment and then grabbed Arwel's arm. 'Come on,' she said, breaking into a run. Arwel followed, and before long they arrived at the sign 'Private Property – Keep Out'. Breathlessly Beth squeezed through the broken railings and up to the entrance to the mine.

They stood in the cold, dark room in front of the mineshaft listening as hard as they could. Arwel thought that he could hear the clank of Number Two's pickaxe, but it could have been the sound of water. 'What are we doing here?' he asked.

'Looking for inspiration – looking for a way to sneak in so the Overman doesn't see us. Could we disguise ourselves?'

They didn't have a torch so both Arwel and Beth turned on their mobile phones. They held them out so that the light spilled into the mine.

'Do we need disguises?' asked Arwel. 'What if we just go in really quietly?' He took a few steps into the mine entrance. Beth followed. Slowly and silently they edged their way forwards into the dark, damp, dank, brick-lined cavern. Water dripped to the floor. The air hung like cold glue in the deep black hole.

Without a sound they crept forwards. Soon they reached the stables and Arwel noticed that there was fresh hay on the floor. He supposed it was where Number Two slept. Now they could clearly hear the clanging of his pickaxe.

'Shush,' whispered Beth, edging futher along the old railway tracks. 'That's him.'

'One thing,' whispered Arwel, 'he won't need to do any training. He'll be as strong as a superhero after all this digging.' He paused, stuck his hand out and leant on a big iron box, some coal-digging machine built by the Overman, he guessed. 'Ooh!' he exclaimed softly. The box was warm to the touch.

From somewhere in the darkness he heard a long-drawn-out shushing noise. And again. 'All right, Beth,' he said. 'You don't have to keep shushing me.'

'I only shushed you once,' said Beth.

'Where did the other shush come from then?'

Too late, he realised that it was the sound of steam rising in a boiler. With another hiss, long, oily steel bars shot out from the sides of the box, catching Arwel between their fingers. He was stuck in a metal claw. 'Get out, Beth!' he yelled, unable to wriggle free. 'Go back.'

'No!' she screamed.

'Get out now, before the Overman comes,' shouted Arwel. 'And don't worry . . . I'll think of something.'

Deep in the mine, Number Two must have heard them. He shouted as loud as he could: 'Get away from this place if you still can!'

In the distance they could hear the approach of the Overman's steam engine as it clanked over ancient tracks.

Beth took one desperate look at Arwel, picked his phone up from the floor and made a dash for it just as the engine hissed into view.

As she ran towards the door she could hear the Overman laughing. 'It's just like the old days,' he said. 'Another volunteer.'

Chapter 15

Beth rushed out of Eight Miles Down. She scrambled past the old brick buildings, through the gap in the fence and only stopped when she got to the other end of Neil Kinnock Avenue. She couldn't think what to do. She sank to the ground, tears slowly filling her eyes. All she could think of was the look on Arwel's face when he realised he was trapped. His eyes were wide with fear. And she was really scared. Arwel's last words were 'I'll think of something'. So far everything he'd thought of had got them deeper and deeper into trouble.

Beth took a deep breath. She stood up. There was nothing for it. She would have to take control of the situation. Before leaving, she shouted as loud as she could towards the mine. 'Don't worry, Arwel. I'll be back.'

*

Aberscary police station was a new building. It was reassuringly bright and clean. Beyond the cream-painted walls of the reception area, through an open door, Beth could see a number of people working. She stood on tiptoe to talk to the desk sergeant, craning her neck to see the map which lay on the counter in front of him.

'Can you point to the place where you say this Arwel disappeared?' asked the sergeant impatiently.

Beth looked at the map. She shook her head. 'The mine's not on the map,' she said. 'I can take you there though.'

'And you say that this boy, Arwel, Mr Rugby's son, was trapped by a steam-powered claw.'

Beth nodded. 'Well, claw-like. It was like these iron bars came shooting out of the sides.' She joined the fingers of both hands together, forming a cage.

'Hmmm,' said the police sergeant.

'It's the Overman from the mine: he's trapped Arwel.'

'This is the one who's taken prisoner both the leg of a zombie and an entire front row forward?'

Beth nodded. 'It's not on the map because the government is scared of anyone finding out the truth.'

'I know,' said the officer. 'You said that bit before.'

'The dark forces,' explained Beth, 'that's why nobody knows the mine's there.'

The sergeant frowned. He folded up the map. 'Well thank you very much for that, miss. We'll make sure that it's on our records. Now, I suggest you hurry home.'

Beth glared at the officer. She knew he didn't believe her. 'I'm telling you, he's been captured,' she shouted, stamping her foot. 'And in case you think I'm wasting your time, I've made a note of your number.'

The officer looked at the clock on the wall. 'Where

do you live, love?' he said wearily. 'You shouldn't really be wandering about at this time of night.'

'I'm not making it up,' shouted Beth. 'There's a crazy engineer in a secret coal mine who thinks our Number Two has to do 36,500 shifts before he can play rugby. And it's not late – it's half past seven.'

'I tell you what,' said the sergeant. 'I'll drive you home. There's a good girl.'

'You think I've lost it. Well I haven't. I've got a good mind to report you. I'll be back to see your superior officer. And thank you, I don't need a lift. I'm quite capable of walking home on my own.'

Beth stormed out of the station and hurried down the street straight to Arwel's house.

*

The Overman pulled a heavy iron lever on the side of Arwel's cage. The finger-like pistons slid open with a hiss of steam and Arwel stepped forwards.

'Pleased to see you, boy. You could have stayed on the surface – but you came back. I don't have much alternative now. You're going to have to dig coal. A lot of coal. How old are you?'

'Thirteen,' said Arwel.

'Old enough,' said the Overman, sliding his grey hand across Arwel's shoulders and grabbing his shirt collar. He dragged Arwel deeper into the mine. Arwel had only ever felt such cold and clammy skin on one other creature – Delme. The Overman, he realised, was a zombie.

*

Beth knocked on Arwel's front door. She was out of breath and worried. She'd run all the way from the police station.

Arwel's mother answered. 'It's Beth, isn't it? I've just put the kettle on. Would you like a biscuit?'

Beth sighed as Dad bounded down the stairs. 'Another confirmation – we're almost there – we've nearly got a team to play.'

Tania appeared in the hall. 'Don't go arranging anything for tomorrow night,' she said.

'Why not?' asked Dad.

'Because it's the theatre night!'

'It's in my BlackBerry,' said Dad, tapping his head. He turned to Beth. 'Hello, girl. You come to see our Arwel? He's not here at the moment.'

'Where is Arwel?' said Tania, moving towards the front door. 'If he misses tomorrow, I'll never speak to him again.'

For a second Beth didn't know what to say. She just stood in the doorway, looking at Arwel's mum, dad and sister. She remembered the police station and how the sergeant had looked at her when she tried to tell the truth. Then she thought about Arwel. Would he really want her to tell about the mine, the zombies and everything? 'Er,' she said.

Arwel's mum held out a saucer with a Rich Tea biscuit on it.

'He asked me to tell you he's having a sleepover – at Martin's.' Beth blurted out the words almost as if she was frightened of them.

'That's fine, so long as Martin's mum doesn't mind. What about his clothes though? His books for tomorrow?'

'That's why I came,' said Beth. 'He asked me to pop around to pick them up.'

'He's staying with his personal trainer,' said Dad. 'They're probably discussing tactics – excellent idea.' He looked at his watch and peered anxiously down the street.

'Yes,' said Beth. 'I'm not interested in all that stuff – that's why I said I'd come over to collect his things. You waiting for someone?'

'Face time,' said Dad. 'Got to see a man about a game.'

Mum sighed and handed the saucer of biscuits to Dad. 'I'll just get his bag,' she said before disappearing upstairs.

Beth nodded.

'Don't you want a biscuit?' said Dad, holding out the saucer.

'Just remember to tell him that he's got to be back here straight after school so that he's got plenty of time to get changed before we go to the show,' called Mum as she hurried upstairs.

Beth nodded again, taking the biscuit. 'No problem,' she said. As she crunched on the Rich Tea a car appeared at the end of the street. Arwel's dad pushed past her onto the pavement.

'At last,' he said. 'How am I looking? Cool, confident, in command?'

Beth nodded as the car pulled up. It wasn't like Steve's Fiesta. It was a shiny red sports car, an Alpha Romeo 8C Spider. The window slid down and a man stuck his head out. 'I'm looking for a guy called Mr Rugby,' he said.

'That's my name. Don't wear it out,' said Dad and a broad smile spread across his face as he recognised the driver.

'I hear you're looking for players,' said the man, 'for a one-off match.'

*

Arwel stood in the orange light of a fire. It glowed through the open hatch of one of the Overman's boilers, deep in Eight Miles Down. Number Two crouched beside him. The air wasn't so cold and damp any more. Warmed by the fires powering the steam engines, it rushed upwards through the ventilation shaft.

'There's no way out,' said Number Two.

Arwel looked around. His foot was chained to the ground. Next to him lay a pickaxe and a shovel.

Nearby was a rusty metal cart into which he had to throw coal. Tied to the cart was a sad-looking little pony blinking in the darkness. Arwel pulled his chain so that he could reach the pony. He patted its mane.

The pony raised its head gently.

'Don't worry,' said Arwel, 'we'll think of something.'

'I've tried everything,' said Number Two, 'but it's impossible – this mine is full of steam power. There are engines everywhere: they trap you, move you on rails and conveyor belts. They've got these metal bars that come steaming out at you.'

'I know,' said Arwel.

The Overman hurried towards them from deep in the tunnel. He held an oil can in one hand and a huge spanner in the other. He pushed his hat back and mopped his brow. 'Pressure's dropping in the main water-pump boiler on level three. It'll take me a few hours to fix it. Are you two just going to stand there talking? Get a move on. We've got targets to meet – quotas to beat.'

Arwel stared at the Overman. There was something vaguely familiar about him.

'I need to show the boy the ropes,' said Number Two.

'Skiving, bunking off, not turning up, not doing your share. In the end everybody suffers and the whole shift misses its target,' shouted the Overman. 'I don't want him to learn any ropes from you. The sooner you realise that we're stuck down here until we hit our quota, the sooner you'll knuckle down to some serious output.'

The Overman pulled an oil-stained pocket watch out of his trouser pocket. It was attached to his belt with an oily piece of string. He looked tired and stressed. The water pumps needed constant attention: without them the mine would flood.

'I'm late. Just dig as much as you can,' said the Overman. 'After I've fixed the boiler I've got to shore up the props on the deep shaft. I haven't got time to talk now, but when I come back, I'll explain the shift patterns.'

'Wait a minute,' said Arwel. 'Are you stuck down here too?'

But the Overman had already rushed into the blackness. His answer echoed back to them. 'I'm one-hundred-per-cent stuck. Correction, with a workforce like you – make that two hundred per cent. If I don't hit my targets, I don't get out, and with you guys up front – well – here's to another hundred years.'

Number Two swung his axe.

Arwel patted the little horse on the nose. 'The Overman's no different to us,' he said. 'He's trapped too, running around all day fixing boilers and props and pumps.'

'Rubbish,' said Number Two, crashing his huge pick into the black coal jagging out of the wall. 'Came to find me, didn't he? He just wants revenge. Busting a gut to reach his targets – the guy's a creep.'

Arwel nodded. 'Years and years of cutting coal . . . with no miners, one little pit pony and some steam engines that probably use up more coal than he can actually dig,' he said. 'He's got no chance.'

'Correction,' said Number Two slowly, swinging his axe. 'We've got no chance.'

'First we've got to break through these chains, and then we've got to find a way to the surface,' said Arwel.

Number Two grunted.

The pony took a few steps, dragging the truck with it. Number Two shouted at it to stop.

'Don't take it out on the little horse,' Arwel said. 'He's been down here for years as well. He probably wants to get out of here as much as we do, don't you, boy?'

The pony neighed softly and scraped the ground. Arwel leant across to see what it was doing. He reached out and patted the horse's nose with his hand. He could see some tools lying beside the coalface. There were hammers, axes, shovels and saws for cutting pit props. Behind the tools, leaning against the wall, was something Arwel recognised – Gryff Griffiths's missing leg.

'Listen,' said Arwel as he patted the pony again. 'I don't know if you can understand me, but if you could reach that saw and kick it over to me it would be a good start.'

Whether the pony understood or not, it began to

nudge the saw with its nose. Slowly the saw moved closer to Arwel.

Number Two looked at Arwel. 'He never done that for me when I asked him.'

Chapter 16

Back at school, Beth joined Glen and Martin at the baseball hoop. Glen passed her the ball. She threw it and it bounced off the side of the hoop.

'Where's Arwel?' asked Glen.

'Has he been grounded too?' said Martin.

Beth felt terrible. Being trapped underground was a whole lot worse than being grounded, she decided. She sighed. She was going to have to trust Martin and Glen. 'Sit down,' she said.

They sat down on the tarmac.

She took a deep breath. Then she held out the mobile phone. 'This is all that's left of Arwel,' she said.

Glen looked at the phone. 'If I call him, will he speak to me?'

'I don't think she means he's in the phone,' said Martin. 'I think she means that the rest of him is somewhere else.'

Then Beth explained.

'What are we going to do?' asked Glen.

Martin shook his head.

'I dunno,' said Beth. 'We've got to think of something.'

But they couldn't think of anything.

*

The rest of the day passed in a terrible daze for Beth. She couldn't concentrate and she wandered from class to class. She'd lied to Arwel's parents about where he was. She'd even texted his mum a message when she asked how the sleepover at Martin's had gone.

'Great,' she'd written. She felt really bad.

She knew they'd find out after school, when Arwel didn't go home. He'd miss the show and then they'd discover that he'd disappeared off the face of the planet.

By half past three Beth was in a real panic. She didn't know where to go or who to talk to. In the end she decided the only thing she could do was go to Arwel's parents and tell them that their son was no longer on the map.

When she arrived she found the place in a state of happy panic. Dad, resplendent in his suit, was leaning against Steve's Fiesta, talking to rugby agents on his phone.

'BlackBerry me,' he kept saying.

Steve and Tania scurried about, putting the finishing touches to their outfits and Mum made tea for anyone who looked as if they needed some.

'Where is he?' demanded Tania, suddenly catching sight of Beth.

Beth couldn't answer the question. She began to cry.

Dad rushed over, closely followed by Steve. 'What's up, Beth?' they asked.

But Beth couldn't stop crying long enough to answer.

'It's Arwel,' said Tania. 'He's done something, hasn't he? He's going to spoil it all. She's come to tell us.'

'It's not like you think,' Beth wailed. 'He didn't mean it.'

At that moment Mum came rushing out into the street. 'Where's Arwel?' she cried. 'What's happened to Arwel?'

Dad put his phone away. A look of concern crossed his face. 'What is it, Beth? Where's the boy?'

Beth just went on crying.

'Where did he go last night?' asked Tania suspiciously. 'Was he really with Glen and that Martin creep?'

Beth shook her head. 'It's terrible,' she said. 'You won't believe how terrible it is!'

Panic began to take hold. Dad began to shout: 'Where's my boy? Where's Arwel?'

Steve tried to talk to Beth calmly, asking her when she'd last seen him.

Mum rushed inside to call the school.

Tania just looked furious. 'In case you've all forgotten, we're supposed to be going to the theatre. Arwel is not going to spoil it again.'

But there was no way they could go. Not without Arwel. Anything could have happened to him. Beth was led into the kitchen and given compulsory biscuits and tea.

'Calm down!' screamed Dad.

'I can't,' she sobbed.

'They're not answering,' said Mum, putting the phone down. 'Just tell us where he is, Beth.'

'I don't know. Well, I do know, but you won't believe me.'

Tania slammed her hand down hard on the table. 'Stop blubbing and spill the beans,' she bellowed.

The words cut through the mayhem. Everyone fell silent. Beth sniffed. She took a big breath. 'I don't think you'll be going to Cardiff tonight,' she began. 'Arwel's . . .'

'. . . here,' said Arwel, standing at the kitchen door, slightly out of breath. 'Sorry I'm late.'

The noise erupted again. Beth cried even harder. Mum pushed Arwel upstairs to get changed. Dad got back on his phone. Steve clenched his fist as if he'd just scored a try. And Tania muttered under her breath: 'Drama queen.'

An hour later, everybody – apart from Beth – was in the Fiesta, dressed up and driving to Cardiff. Arwel, squeezed in the back seat, decided it was best to keep quiet about his escape from Eight Miles Down.

The rest of them, even Mum, had a wonderful evening. But in the theatre, when the lights dipped low, all Arwel could think about was Number Two clanging his pick into the coalface in time with the music.

The musical ended with a big finale that had the audience joining in with the chorus. Tania and Steve knew the words and sang along enthusiastically. Even Arwel clapped in time with the music. His dad stood up and cheered. Mum laughed and applauded too. She said it was the best night out she'd had for years.

'Thank you, everybody,' said Tania, when, finally, they pulled up in the Fiesta outside the hotel.

Chapter 17

The following afternoon, Arwel was back in the school library. The smell of curry was still there. But Beth seemingly wasn't. He looked in the usual places, the issue desk, the computer terminals, the low coffee table with its saggy bean bags. Eventually he found her sitting in a dark corner, reading.

'We've got to talk,' he said.

'I'm not speaking to you.'

'Why not?'

'Because you're treating me like an idiot.'

'I know how to get Number Two out of the mine.'

'Do I care?' said Beth. 'This has gone far enough – you're making us all look like fools. I'm in trouble with my mum. You're in trouble with school for mitching off. Glen and Martin are grounded and now they've got detention.'

'I was stuck in a haunted coal mine. I only managed to get out by sawing through my chains. I found an airshaft and I scraped my way out,' moaned Arwel.

'Why didn't you bring Number Two with you?'

'He was too big to fit through the hole. I tried everything,' said Arwel, 'but we can get him out. We just need to try one more time.'

Beth shook her head, too angry to speak.

'Shall we watch a film this evening at your place, a zombie film?'

'No,' said Beth. 'Go away.'

Arwel hung around for a while, but Beth seemed determined to ignore him. She stared at her book until he moved away. 'And another thing,' she shouted after him.

Arwel paused at the door.

'You could have asked me if I'd have liked to see the show. You lot all went off in that car without a thought for me. Did you have a nice time?'

Arwel pushed through the door and stepped back out into the long corridor. Somehow he'd managed to offend everybody.

*

Arwel stayed away from the forest that night. He didn't go the next night, or the night after that. Whenever he thought about the Overman trying to hit his impossible targets, the zombies training for a game they couldn't win, Martin and Glen grounded, and Beth not speaking to him, he shivered and tried to concentrate on something else. The worst times were after he'd gone to sleep. He dreamt about the pony and Number Two, deep underground, working by the light of a glowing boiler, laboriously cutting tons and tons of coal.

Then one morning in the kitchen, Dad tapped him on the shoulder. 'We're ready,' he said.

Arwel was eating a piece of toast. He held it up in front of his face. 'Talk to the toast.'

Dad grabbed it and took a big bite. 'Boy, this is important,' he said, spluttering crumbs. 'It's on.'

'What d'you mean?' asked Arwel.

'We've got a team to play, and a ground. It's game on,' he said, popping his mobile phone into his pocket.

'Oh,' said Arwel, as if his dad was talking about a trip to the supermarket.

'I don't think you quite get it. I'm done with BlackBerries and business – now it's time for action. Come with me.'

Dad led him from the living room, through the hall and into the street.

'What are we doing out here?'

'Just wait a second,' said Dad.

A bright red Alpha Romeo appeared at the end of Constellation Street. It was the. Its engine buzzed sweetly as it slid up to Arwel's house. The window slipped down and the man inside spoke. 'Hop in, you two.'

In a couple of minutes they were zooming down the motorway, Arwel crammed in the tiny back seat, while his dad and the driver discussed international players, television deals and 'the game'. The driver had white curly hair and spoke with a strange accent. Dad called him 'mate'. He seemed to know him quite well.

'Me and your dad, we go back a long way, Arwel. In

the old days we met a few times on the pitch . . . when New Zealand were on tour.'

'Are you an All Black?' asked Arwel.

'Once you wear the jersey,' laughed the man, 'you can't get it off.'

Arwel's jaw dropped.

'Bob's a promoter. He manages a big team. He's helping me,' said Dad. 'Before that, he played for New Zealand.'

'Your dad's a great fellow,' said the All Black. 'When he said he had a team called the Zombies who needed a game, well I couldn't say no, could I?'

They screeched off the motorway and soon they came to a halt outside a huge new stadium. Arwel and his dad gasped as they stepped out of the sports car.

'This is the ground,' said Bob. 'Got a deal with the TV lot – you're going to be all over the world.'

'Nice one,' said Dad.

Arwel felt a buzz of excitement. The ground was full of people preparing for the opening game. Huge trucks arrived, carrying TV cables and satellite dishes, and everybody seemed to know his dad.

'Not bad, eh,' whispered Dad to Arwel as they stepped out onto the pitch, 'for a former member of the Aberscary committee?'

Arwel gasped again. Rows of seats rose from the pitch. Under the floodlights, which were under test, ground staff poked the green grass with forks.

'I can't wait to see the first game,' said Arwel.

'You're not going to "see" anything,' smiled Dad. 'You're playing.'

'No way,' said Arwel, as they walked out onto the neatly mown pitch.

'We've got international players from all over the world,' said Bob the All Black as he followed them onto the turf. 'Your dad and I were able to call in quite a lot of favours.'

'It won't be a real international match,' said Dad, 'but it'll give your boys and the Aberscary committee something to think about.'

'What's the team going to be called?' asked Arwel. He started to jog on the grass. He felt good, confident – like he had before.

'They're an invitation fifteen – they don't have a name. You can't just make a rugby team: they're all tied into contracts and stuff, but for a favour for a mate, you can still pull something off.'

After the tour of the ground the All Black drove them home. He shook Arwel by the hand. 'Looking forward to kick-off,' he said. 'It was a pleasure to meet you, Arwel. Your dad tells me you're magic on the pitch.'

Arwel laughed nervously. 'When are we playing?' he asked.

'Wednesday, evening kick-off. They say your boys play better after dark.'

With that, the Alpha Romeo 8C Spider slipped

out of Constellation Street, leaving Arwel and his dad standing on the pavement. For a while, they didn't say anything, both lost in their own thoughts.

'We got a Lamborghini Gallardo up in the forest,' muttered Arwel softly.

*

'The boys will be really happy, Arwel,' said Delme later that evening. 'They've been getting a bit restless. But how are we going to manage without Number Two? We're a zombie short of a team. And Gryff's still minus a leg.'

'I'm working on it,' said Arwel. 'Just make sure you keep up with the training. We've got until Wednesday.'

He didn't sound convincing, even to himself.

Chapter 18

The next few days at Arwel's were even crazier than usual. The phone didn't stop ringing. News people from the TV and the newspapers kept knocking on the door, and rugby players, really famous ones, kept arriving, often in sports cars. They came to see Dad. Even Tania was getting excited.

On Wednesday morning Dad arrived in the kitchen. 'This is it,' he said, pouring hot water onto a teabag in a mug. 'No more face time – it's rugby time from here on in. Are you and the boys ready?'

Arwel nodded slowly. It was the day of the game. He hadn't seen the zombies since speaking to Delme, Beth still wasn't talking to him and Glen and Martin had only just been allowed back out. He wasn't ready. 'We'll be ready,' he said quietly, before hurrying off to school.

*

Arwel found himself standing outside the changing rooms, looking at the team sheets. He could hear Mr Edwards doing his team talk. 'One-hundred-per-cent effort, boys; correction, one-hundred-and-ten per cent.'

Arwel thought he sounded like the Overman,

but less threatening. They even looked a bit like one another.

At that moment, Glen arrived. He slapped Arwel on the back, making him jump. Martin appeared, punching Arwel in a friendly way.

'It's tonight then,' said Martin.

'You got a full team?' asked Glen.

They were excited. News about the game had filtered through. And they were both, finally, ungrounded.

Arwel shook his head. 'Not a complete team, no bus to take us to the ground, no nothing really.'

He could see Beth walking down the corridor, holding a newspaper.

'I see the Zombies are playing tonight,' she said, pointing to the sports pages.

Arwel shook his head again. 'It'll have to be thirteen men and uncontested scrums,' he said. 'I don't think it'll be worth turning up for. We're going to get mashed – have you seen who they've got playing for them?'

They read through the list of players Dad and his New Zealand mate had put together. Players came from all over the world: Australia, France, Argentina, England, Scotland, Ireland and Wales. At the end of the list was his dad's name, followed by the title 'Chairman of the Rugby Zombies Committee and Head of Sports Development'.

'A lot of people from school are going,' said Beth.

'A lot of people from all over the place are going,' said Martin.

'Shame Number Two is still stuck in a hole in the ground,' said Glen.

'Have you got new kit sorted out?' asked Beth.

Arwel hadn't thought about that. He shook his head.

'Trainer? Physio? Manager? Coach?' asked Martin.

'Well, you've been grounded and Beth's not talking to me. I don't know anybody else,' said Arwel.

'So what exactly is your plan?'

'Collect the zombies at six o'clock, catch a bus, play rugby, get mashed, catch a bus home,' said Arwel.

Gilligan walked past. 'I'm going to watch your team tonight, Arwel. It's going to be hilarious,' he said. 'You lot are going to come back here by ambulance.' Gilligan chuckled at his joke as he strutted into the changing rooms.

'He's right,' said Arwel. 'My dad's been wearing the same suit for a week, he drives around in a sports car with this New Zealand guy and he's completely forgotten about the team he's supposed to be representing. They're going to destroy us.'

'You'd better come with us,' said Martin.

'Where? Are we going to run away?' asked Arwel hopefully.

'There's nowhere to run,' said Beth, with a wink.

'Let's take him to the art department,' said Glen, as they made their way down the long corridor.

'Look, whatever you've been doing in there, I'm not interested. Whilst you've been splodging paint on walls, connecting up with your inner feelings, I've been out there trying to deal with zombies and their problems,' snapped Arwel. 'They're really seriously messed up.'

'It's not like you think,' said Beth as they turned off the long corridor and walked up the short flight of stairs that led to the art room. She pushed the door and they walked in. There, on the table, was a pile of rugby jerseys.

Glen picked one and held it up. 'I designed it myself,' he said proudly.

The shirt was black with a grey skeleton-pattern on the front. On the back it said 'zombies' in big red letters above the number.

'Wow!' said Arwel. 'They're amazing.'

'It's surprising how much you can do during a few hours' detention, if you put your mind to it,' said Beth, holding a shirt up like a dress and swaying around the room.

'How many have you got?' asked Arwel.

'Plenty,' said Martin, 'enough for the team and the coaching staff. We didn't want to go on telly looking like we don't know what we're doing.'

'It was Beth's idea,' said Glen. 'We got done for mitching so Beth suggested we did needlework. The teachers thought this would be an excellent punishment.'

'I just came and showed them how to do it,' said Beth.

'But you didn't have detention,' said Arwel.

'Call it voluntary work. I was helping the disadvantaged,' she said with a smile.

Glen and Martin grinned. They didn't mind Beth making jokes about them. If it had been anybody else, they would have mashed them.

'We've got kit, banners, hats, the lot, even dog biscuits – we don't want them going exfrastic again,' said Martin. 'Help me stick them in this box and we'll take them up to the team after school.'

*

When Delme and the others saw the kit their eyes lit up. They'd been practising hard, just as Arwel had asked. They knew the game was on. They were as ready as they could be.

Gryff Griffiths hopped over to Arwel. 'Look,' he said, seriously. 'I'm not so fast on one leg, and I definitely can't sidestep, but I can still tackle.'

Arwel patted Gryff on the back. He didn't know what to say. He thought that Gryff was possibly the bravest zombie he'd ever met.

Delme interrupted him. 'Fourteen players are better than none, Arwel. We're here for you.'

The zombies loved their kit. Once they were all wearing the special jerseys even Arwel felt different.

'OK, everyone,' said Delme. 'Time for a little jog. Beth, Martin and Glen, hop on the second row. Arwel, jump up – we're going to run down to the ground. It's about twenty miles. We'll be there in plenty of time.'

'Wait!' shouted Arwel. 'We can't go yet. There's something we've got to do.'

Delme looked at his team, and at Beth, Martin and Glen. They were all ready to go.

'Before we do it, I need to say something,' said Arwel. 'Our team motto. Remember? One for all and all for one.'

'What's he talking about?' asked Glen.

'*The Three Musketeers* by Alexander Dumas,' said Beth, 'although I don't think he knows that.'

'In this team we don't drop anyone. We stick together,' said Arwel. 'Follow me.'

Chapter 19

As crowds began to pour into the ground, Dad was greeting the players in the car park. He looked up as a helicopter slowly descended. That was the invitation outside half.

Bob stood nearby, looking smart in his New Zealand blazer. 'There doesn't seem to be any sign of the opposing team.'

'Don't worry about Arwel,' said Dad. 'His boys like to make an entrance. They'll be here, don't you worry.'

*

Once they'd arrived at Eight Miles Down, Arwel led the zombies past the railings at the mine entrance and on to the scramble hole through which he'd escaped. It led to the pony, to the missing leg, to Number Two . . . and to the Overman.

The zombies muttered as Arwel explained his plan. They were kitted up already in their new jerseys and didn't want to listen. All they wanted to do was play rugby. They were also scared of the Overman and his battery of steam-powered defences. Some of them had been colliers and feared that they might be put to work forever in the mine.

But Arwel was adamant. 'You can't play without a hooker, not properly. It says so in the laws. Whether you like it or not, we've got to get Number Two out. Remember I told you I'd think of a plan? Well I've done it. This is what we do. Someone get me a rope. And start digging – we've got to widen this hole so that it's big enough for Number Two and a horse to fit through. After that, we split up. Beth, Glen and Martin will take the pack to the mine entrance – the backs can work the rope.'

*

Dad had taken his place in the dugout in the ground. The floodlights shone, casting a silvery light over the thousands of people packing the stadium. He couldn't believe his eyes. He waved up at Mum. She was sitting with Tania and Steve near the halfway line.

Bob sat next to Dad. 'Not bad going, Mr Rugby. They don't know what they're missing, that committee of yours.'

A short man in a long woolly coat and a flat cap tugged at Dad's sleeve. 'Do you mind if I join you?' asked Benbow. 'The whole of Aberscary rugby club and committee are up there,' he said, smiling. 'Rows ZB 145 to ZZ 330. They've never seen anything like this.'

Dad beamed and stared up into the stands, but he couldn't make out any of the faces.

'I hope you don't mind me coming along,' said Benbow. 'I don't think I've ever missed a game.'

'You sure you wouldn't prefer to be with the boys up there?'

'Nope,' said Benbow. 'I'm with you. Although I must say, I think the purple shirt is a bit over the top.'

Dad ignored the comment – he knew his outfit was good. 'Dress to impress,' he said. 'You want to take on the world – you've got to look like you know what you're doing.'

Benbow eyed him up and down. 'You look splendid,' he said, 'and your team is awesome. If a little elusive. Where are they?'

'Don't worry,' said Dad.

On the emerald turf the invitation fifteen jogged, kicked and passed the ball. The forwards charged at tackle bags, crunching them out of the way.

Television cameras practised their moves around the touchline and in the press boxes reporters switched on their microphones and began broadcasting.

In one of the most extraordinary games of the modern era, a small Welshman, from an unheard-of town : . . I'm sorry, let me get that right, an unheard-of Welshman from a small town deep in the Welsh valleys has pulled off an extraordinary coup. After forty years of unstinting service to Aberscary rugby club, Mr Rugby has finally hit the big time. By calling on his many friends from all over the world, he has been able to gather together a star-studded team to take on an unknown quantity: the Rugby Zombies. Not much is known about them – where they come from or who they are. It is rumoured that their outside half is just thirteen years old. It's also said that they play as if they come from a different world. Whatever the explanation behind their phenomenon, there can be no doubt that this team of mysterious strangers has captured the imagination of the rugby-going public. Tonight promises to be a very special occasion.

*

'On my call,' shouted Arwel as four of the zombies lowered him into the ventilation shaft. The rope creaked and swung as they paid out more and more. Finally it went slack. Arwel had reached the coalface. He shouted and one word echoed up the shaft. 'Now!'

Up at the surface the backs heard the call and shouted down the valley: 'Now!'

From the safety of Neil Kinnock Avenue, Martin heard the shout and yelled: 'Now!'

Beth, stationed at the entrance to Eight Miles Down, heard the shout and raced to the room at the pithead where the pack had gathered. 'Now!' she yelled.

'No need to shout,' said Delme. 'Some of us have still got ears.' Then he turned to the forwards and bellowed: 'Right, you lot. Form up! Prepare to charge!'

*

Meanwhile Arwel had crawled back from the shaft to the place where Number Two was working. He tapped him on the shoulder, made a sign for him to drop his shovel and handed him the rope. Then Arwel found the pony and led it by its harness to the airshaft. Soon he heard the terrible roars of the Overman's engine mingling with shouts and screams from the zombies. It was an unholy commotion. The diversion was working. The Overman and his steam engines were fully occupied.

*

The clock ticked on. The commentators were running out of things to say. There were now no players on the pitch. For the seventh time, the TV commentator ran through the team-sheet for the invitation fifteen:

> From Ireland we have the unstoppable centres. They'll be keen to make their mark on the game; from France, the second row: giants of men; from Australia, from England, from everywhere...but they're not on the pitch at the moment. In fact the pitch is empty. As yet – we don't have two teams. Some of the crowd are getting restless. They've started a slow handclap.

Down in the dugout, Bob and Dad exchanged nervous glances. Benbow tried to reassure him but he could see that his friend from New Zealand wasn't pleased at all. He kept checking his watch and shaking his head.

*

'Pull!' shouted Arwel.

At the top of the shaft, Gryff with his two centres, pulled as hard as they could on the rope leading down the ventilation shaft. It began to inch upwards.

Finally, to everyone's delight, Number Two and the pit pony emerged from the shaft, closely followed by Arwel. 'Come on!' he yelled, throwing a jersey at Number Two. 'There's no time to lose. Get that on. You've got a game to play.'

Number Two laughed as he pulled the jersey over his massive shoulders. 'Just like the old days,' he grinned.

The little pony blinked in the half-light. Arwel grabbed the rope that hung from his neck. 'I hope you don't mind carrying this,' he whispered in the pony's ear, slinging a bin bag across his back.

The pony dipped its head and they all began to make their way towards the mine entrance. The pony, dazzled by the accustomed light, breathed the fresh air, neighing and whinnying with pleasure.

When they arrived at the pithead Arwel could see the zombie forwards were in trouble. The Overman was right behind them. Delme and his pack were howling in pain and fury as flashes of fire streaked the billowing smoke and steam.

'Get out of there!' yelled Arwel. 'Come on!'

The zombies didn't need telling twice. They emerged, spluttering, covered in soot.

Close behind them stood the Overman. He snarled when he spotted Number Two in his new jersey. 'One hundred years have passed and you're still sneaking off work to play rugby. You know what, Number Two? You'll never make anything of yourself.'

Number Two shrugged his shoulders. 'I wasn't made to live underground!'

The Overman roared with rage, and sprang back onto his steam engine. He started to pull at the big brass levers. But instead of advancing, the engine slid suddenly backwards, leaving a trail of black soot hanging in the air. As it disappeared into the depths of the mine, they could hear the Overman's despairing shout: 'I'll bring you back – and this time it won't just be that Number Two – all of you owe me time. Every zombie, every pony, every child will work double time in this mine until we reach the target. I'll get my colliers back, just you wait and see.'

Delme waved his hand as if swatting a fly. 'Climb on my shoulders, Arwel. We're late.'

*

The All Black turned to Mr Rugby. 'Have you been wasting my time? I'm a plain-speaking man and I don't like to look a fool. Where are the Zombies?'

Stewards had walked onto the pitch. The crowd booed and hissed as an announcement came over the PA system. 'We apologise for the delay. In the event that tonight's game is cancelled a full refund will be given.'

Dad looked around desperately. Last time the Rugby Zombies had arrived fashionably late. This time, he thought, they'd taken things too far. He thought about the Aberscary committee – laughing at him up in rows ZB 145 to ZZ 330.

Benbow pulled his sleeve. 'I don't want to seem disloyal, but if we sneak out now, we might be able to make it back home without getting beaten up.'

Dad crouched in his bunker. He wasn't going anywhere.

*

For Arwel, perched on Delme's shoulders, the run was the most amazing experience of his entire life. He was sure it must be for Beth, Glen and Martin too, as they sped towards the ground on the backs of charging zombies. Gryff took the pit pony in his Lamborghini and followed the route cut by the leaders. They whizzed overland like bullets. They swerved around corners; when they couldn't swerve they simply smashed. Arwel could hear the screams of the others as they crashed through concrete walls, jumped over rivers and flew along the dark streets. They were like a pack of wolves spreading across the night.

When they arrived at the stadium, the crowd had started to leave, grumbling as they clogged the exits.

There was no time to lose. Arwel and the others leapt off the zombies' backs and Gryff led the pony out of the sports car. They formed up into two lines and then Arwel, taking the pony's leading rope, headed the procession into the players' entrance.

'What's with the pony, Arwel?' asked Beth. 'He can't play.'

'Every team has a mascot,' said Arwel. 'This is ours.'

'Has he got a name?' asked Beth.

The pony shook his head.

'I don't suppose he has,' said Arwel. 'He was very unlucky to have such a miserable owner.'

'*Unlucky*,' repeated Beth thoughtfully. 'That makes sense if you're a zombie mascot.' She patted the little pony, who seemed almost to be smiling. 'But I think we'll call you "Lucky". It's time you started enjoying yourself.'

Arwel could tell that the pony couldn't see very well. The bright floodlights made no difference to him. He just walked calmly forwards.

The announcer was just about to call the game off. Dad and Bob were arguing with each other in the dugout. The players from the international fifteen were sitting on the grass, waiting to go home, and half the stadium was already empty when Arwel stepped out onto the pitch with Lucky. The zombies, resplendent in their skeleton shirts, followed close behind. Arwel blinked in the floodlights and looked around.

The crowd fell silent, the announcer stopped talking and even the reporters in the press boxes didn't know what to say. The Rugby Zombies had arrived: they were speech-defying.

'They've got a horse,' spluttered the announcer. 'They're here, and I have to say I have never seen such an ugly-looking team. Their wing three-quarter has only one leg.'

Way up in one of the stands, someone started to clap. Gradually others followed suit until the whole ground was a cauldron of noise. The seats filled up again and someone threw Arwel the ball. But before he kicked off, he remembered something and put the ball down on the pitch. He pulled the black bin bag off Lucky's back and rushed over to Gryff, who was balancing precariously on one leg. Trying not to draw attention to himself, he produced Gryff's missing limb. 'I hope you didn't think I'd forgotten this.'

'Well,' said Gryff. 'I didn't like to ask.' He shoved his leg back on and wiggled it around. 'That's better,' he said.

'Correction,' said the announcer. 'The wing three-quarter now has two legs.'

Martin led Lucky to the bunker. Someone tossed the ball to Arwel. He held it high for everyone to see. The crowd cheered and roared. They'd waited a long time for this. Some of them had had to rush back to their seats from the car park.

Arwel wiped the ball on his shirt. He smiled as he remembered how bad he'd felt the last time he kicked off. He looked ahead of him. Fifteen of the world's best rugby players were ranged in front of him. They looked angry: they didn't like to be kept waiting.

Chapter 20

Bang! Arwel kicked the ball and it soared high into the night sky, hanging in the air like a gull waiting to dive. The zombie pack led by Delme and Number Two roared into the attack. Number Two felt the clean air fill his lungs. He spat out the black coal dust. The pack advanced like a Challenger tank. Number Two laughed: this was what he liked to do. This was what he was made for. The ball was poised perfectly: after holding the air like a weightless feather, it dropped like a bomb.

*

Delme leapt off the ground and palmed the ball back down to Number Two, who caught it with both hands and drove at the opponents' pack. He felt the two zombie props join him like pieces of a well-fitting jigsaw. They crunched forwards until the weight of the tacklers pulled them down. With a delicate flick of his hand, Number Two popped the ball backwards for the scrum half to pick up. In one seamless movement he dived, scooped and spun the ball to Arwel.

Arwel could see the two opposing flankers bearing down on him, their outside half in front and the centres closing him down. He took two steps forward, jinked to his left, sending one tackler flying, then sped towards the gap between the centres. Gryff Griffiths cut in from the wing and Arwel deftly flipped him the ball. He carried on running towards the right wing. Gryff, knowing Arwel would cover his position, jinked back and passed the ball to one of the centres. The centre took the tackle and spun the ball to his partner, who took the next tackle, and almost lost control of the ball. But with the tips of his fingers he managed to pass it out into space on the right wing. Arwel grabbed the ball and ran. Now there was just the opposing winger and the full-back to beat. He knew Gryff and his centres were still on the ground. But he knew the pack was following him. If he could find Delme they could drive over the line.

Arwel heard a voice. 'Inside!' Without thinking, he flipped the ball inside just as the winger and the full-back flattened him.

The ball hung in the air. It looked as if it was going to be gathered by the opposition. But here was Number Two steaming up like a train. He grabbed the ball and bulldozed his way to the line.

Five nil.

Arwel made swift work of the conversion kick. Up went the touch judges' flags. The crowd roared.

In the dugout, Martin, Beth and Glen jumped into the air. 'Yes!' they shouted.

'He's back on form,' yelled Martin. 'You see what I mean? If you think you're gonna lose, you lose; and if you think you're gonna win . . .'

Lucky munched the grass, raising an eyebrow to see what all the fuss was about.

'They're brilliant!' shouted Glen.

Beth smiled as Gryff trotted past. His leg seemed to be holding up pretty well.

Arwel, although he was by far the smallest person on the pitch, felt like a giant. As big as Delme. He took one moment to look around. The bright lights seemed to coat everything with a silvery glow. He could see Dad in his fancy suit talking excitedly to Benbow; he could see Glen, Martin and Beth cheering and shouting; he could see Lucky sensing the excitement; he could feel twenty thousand fans screaming for more. He tried to register the moment. He wanted to remember how brilliant everything was.

Delme trotted past him. 'Concentrate, boy. The game's not over yet.'

*

Benbow tugged on Mr Rugby's arm. 'Nice one! That's their fifth try.'

Dad punched the air as his friend, the All Black, leant across. 'Sorry about my little outburst earlier,' he said. 'Your boy's got an incredible team. You were right.'

The zombies were playing out of their skins, or what was left of them. Their passes flew like arrows and their kicks pinged down the lines with pinpoint accuracy: a team so fast, powerful – and quite simply brilliant – that nothing could stop them.

'Zombies, Zombies, Zombies!' chanted the crowd.

For a second Arwel looked up. He felt sure he could even hear his sister's voice joining in with the chant.

'Listen,' said the All Black, as one of the invitation fifteen was stretchered off in the final minute. 'These Rugby Zombies are good enough to play the best team in the world.'

Dad's expression changed. 'Wales?' he said. 'We could never get that game.'

'New Zealand!' said the All Black. 'Get your boy and his zombies to New Zealand. We'll give 'em a real international!'

Epilogue

Arwel, Beth, Martin and Glen sat on the wall, watching a Euro-Freight truck make its way south through the misty orange glow on the dual carriageway.

'We won,' said Glen. 'I can't believe it.'

'Nor can I,' said Arwel.

'You were brilliant,' said Martin.

'Not just brilliant,' said Beth, 'unbelievably, incredibly brilliant. Never-seen-anything-like-it-and-never-going-to-see-anything-like-it-again brilliant.'

'Your dad went crazy. He almost got thrown out of the ground,' said Martin. 'He kissed the pony.'

Lucky, who was munching grass nearby, snorted.

'Even the Aberscary committee was cheering,' said Arwel.

Glen watched the truck disappear. 'I hope the zombies weren't in there, going off on another bender. I don't think I could do all that again.'

'They're not,' said Arwel. 'They're working. Getting rid of all that crazy energy they create when they win.'

'Working?' asked Martin.

'Call it flexitime,' said Beth. 'My mum works...'

'Yeah we know: your mum works for the council,' said Martin.

'I don't want to worry you, Arwel,' said Glen,

'but now you're going to play at outside half in a full international.'

Arwel looked at the others. Suddenly he leapt off the wall and started jumping around, punching the air. 'We did it!'

The others joined him, their cries echoing through the still, cool, empty pinewoods behind them.

*

Deep underground, fourteen zombies, still wearing their new rugby jerseys, finished the job Number Two had started over a hundred years previously. In one night, with their bare hands, they pulled 36,500 days' worth of coal from the ground.

And in the morning, before the sun rose, they were back in the forest, finally free to take on their greatest challenge. The Last International.